FLOCK OF WOLVES

SYDNEY RYE MYSTERIES
BOOK 10

EMILY KIMELMAN

Heading illustration: Autumn Whitehurst
Cover Design: Christian Bentulan
Formatting: Jamie Davis

For Jamie and Toby: powerful women who have inspired and challenged me since I met them. I wouldn't be the writer or businesswoman I am without you.
Thank you.

I am time, the destroyer of all; I have come to consume the world.
—Krishna-Dwaipayana Vyasa, *Bhagavad Gita*

HER PROPHET

Bleeding doesn't frighten me. I bleed every *month*. I am the fucking creator. You can take nothing from me because I am life. I am existence. I am you.
I am Her.

CHAPTER ONE
I WILL SURVIVE

Sydney

The doctor flashed her penlight into my eyes, and I blinked against the bright ray. My dog Blue sat on the floor next to me, his head resting on my knee. My fingers curled around the edge of the exam table, gripping onto the seat, hoping I could hold onto reality.

Robert Maxim stood by the door, his arms crossed and face shadowed. He watched us, reminding me of a simmering pot, one just on the cusp of a rolling boil.

The sound of thunder rumbled in the back of my brain. The stringent scent of the hospital tickled my nose. My heart echoed in my chest, pounding out Mulberry's name.

He'd changed my life, Mulberry—helped me when I needed it and when I didn't. Touched me when I asked and stayed away when I insisted. Now, if my mind was to be believed, his life teetered on the edge, his leg blown off, the veins opened, his blood spilled onto the battlefield, rushing away from him.

I should be the one dying.

I should be dead.

The doctor stepped back, a woman in her early 40s with straight black hair and big glasses that slipped down her elegant little nose. "You've suffered major trauma."

Thanks Captain Obvious.

"I think…" She cocked her head, narrowing her eyes, inspecting me like a gardener might a plant that refused to grow toward the sun. "We need to get you back to the States." She turned to Robert.

Thunder rumbled louder, crackling in my ears and blotting out her voice. Lightning sizzled across my vision, and I blinked against the bright, white light.

A woman's voice whispered through the storm…*You are a miracle.*

I shook my head, trying to shake free of the hallucinations, but they clung to me like fog hovering over a harbor—thick and dangerous, but intangible, impossible to touch or avoid. There and yet not.

Had my worst nightmare really come true? Mulberry, the man I loved, in dire danger. Me, powerless to help.

I stayed away to keep him safe.

Everyone I love dies.

Blue scooted closer, his weight warm and welcome against my leg. I rubbed one of his velvety ears.

According to Robert Maxim, Blue had fathered puppies. I glanced up at the man, blinking away the shards of light still crisscrossing my pupils.

Robert spoke to the doctor, his expression calm and controlled, like he owned the world. Like nothing in it could hurt him.

I could.

That's what that simmer was about—that anger bubbling just below the flat surface of Robert Maxim. It pissed him off that I existed, and he didn't own me.

I looked at Blue. Did I own him? *No.* We were partners, connected in a way that left me tethered here. Attached to this world. As tall as a Great Dane, with the long, elegant snout of a collie and the thick coat and markings of a wolf, with one blue eye and one brown, Blue made this feel real.

The doctor left, and Robert turned to me. He crossed his arms again. "Tell me what you remember."

I held his gaze, the blue-green of a gentle, yet dangerous sea...deceptively cold. The kind of water that, if you fell in, would freeze you so fast you'd hardly realize you were dying.

Was I dying?

"I need to speak with Dan or Merl."

I trusted Dan and Merl. They didn't want anything from me...not like Maxim. They'd know what to do.

Robert's lips thinned for a moment before he spoke. "So, you remember them?"

"Of course I do," I frowned.

"And you remember me."

I held his gaze and let a small smile steal over my mouth. "You're awfully hard to forget." His lips pursed, not amused. I sighed and glanced down at Blue, soot and dust from the battle still coating his fur. I'd gotten a shower and a clean set of clothes—lightweight black canvas, the kind of stuff meant for hot weather and dangerous fights.

"We captured Abu Mohammad al-Baghdadi." I glanced up at Robert, and he nodded. Working with the Peshmerga all-female fighting force, led by my friend Zerzan, we captured Abu Mohammad al-Baghdadi—one of the top theologians of Isis, the guy who found passages in the Quran that made it not only okay, but a moral imperative, to bring Sharia law to the world. "And I knew that someone on our team was going to try to kill me."

"Yes." Robert had warned me that the CIA had contracted with one of the men on our team to take me out after we captured al-Baghdadi. "And you refused to listen."

I shrugged. "I listened, and I chose to continue anyway. It was important."

Another flicker of emotion over his face. "Important enough to die for?"

"I wanted to die."

He grunted. "And now?" His voice sounded squeezed, almost like he didn't want to know the answer.

"I don't know what I want. I don't know what happened to me. Robert, I thought I was dead. I was lying there on the ground, bleeding, pretty sure it was all over, and then this woman appeared." I closed my eyes, going back to that moment—it was almost hidden, blocked by pain and trauma, like words on a memorial nearly erased by rain and time. "She stood over me, she had on a burka...and then I was running down that hill, right into that battle."

Robert paced away and then turned back to me, spearing me with a glare from across the room. "So, you don't remember being in a cave?"

I shook my head.

"You don't remember seeing me. Turning away from me?" he asked, his voice remaining flat—as placid as the sea behind his eyes. But I could hear the danger and feel the icy chill of those deep waters threatening to suck me under.

I shook my head again. "What are you talking about?"

"Sydney." He crossed the room quickly, grabbing my hands. His were warm and calloused, and I let him hold me. "I went looking for you." He held my gaze, emotion flickering over the surface of that calm sea, a breeze stirring its glassy surface.

I smiled. "I'm not surprised. You aren't good at letting things go."

"I found you."

"Oh."

"Blue was there, with a pregnant bitch...that's how I knew he had puppies." He looked down at our joined hands. "You turned away from me. And...I didn't go after you. I'm sorry." His voice lowered so that I almost didn't hear him. "I didn't realize that you were under someone else's control."

Hot anger sliced through me. *Under someone else's control? No fucking way.*

"We'll get you back to the States." He kept looking at our joined hands. "The doctors who worked with you in Miami can probably help you again." I shook my head, chasing away the heat of my rage, clearing a line of thinking. I wasn't going anywhere without speaking to Dan or Merl. I trusted them. Robert Maxim could never be trusted. Not entirely.

"I need to speak to Dan."

"You don't trust me?" His voice was the same deep rumble of the thunder that ricocheted inside my brain.

"Nobody trusts you."

His gaze flicked down to Blue, and Robert pulled out his phone, passing it over to me. "Call whoever you want. I'll wait outside."

He gave up too easily.

I took the slim, elegant handset from him, our fingers brushing for the barest of moments. The ghost of a smile curled at the edge of his lips before he gave a curt nod and turned to the door, leaving me alone with Blue.

I looked down at my dog, who sighed and leaned against me. "What do you think?" I asked, but Blue didn't answer.

A voice inside my head whispered...*you can't ever leave me.*

A shiver ran over my body, and I stood up, testing my strength, needing to move, to free myself from the storm inside my mind.

Lightning cracked and thunder rolled, but I held onto myself. *I knew what was real. Didn't I?*

EK

Anita

Dan's black leather couch creaked as he leaned forward and hit play on the laptop.

Through the tinted glass front wall of his office, high above the command center, we could see the giant screen covered in different operations and the operatives at their desks below, but they couldn't see us.

We were in a secret cave.

Dan sat back as the video began, his thigh brushing against mine and his shoulder depressing the back of the couch so that I tipped slightly into him, his body warming my entire side. I created space between us, leaning toward the screen as the video began.

A huge man holding a machete stood on a wooden stage. Before him a crowd jostled. The camera was set up to the side of the stage so that we could see the man's profile. *The Butcher.*

Dan reached forward and turned up the volume as a woman dressed in long black robes was pushed onto the stage from behind the camera.

With the volume raised, I could make out the chanting of the crowd. "Infidel! Infidel! Butcher her!"

The woman—her face swollen with bruises and hair matted with blood—was young, hardly more than a teenager. She stumbled, and the Butcher grabbed her, pulling her into the center of the platform.

He leaned down and spoke to her, but it was impossible to hear him over the rowdy crowd.

Nausea swirled in my gut. I knew where this was going. I'd seen other videos of the Butcher, a famous Isis executioner who specialized in women.

The blade rose into the air and then swung down, whacking into the woman's thigh. The crowd erupted in applause and cheers, leaning toward the violence, the death...the murder.

The young woman hung from the Butcher's hand. Her face turned toward the camera for a moment, possibly looking at someone behind it, a serene smile gracing her split lips.

I cleared my throat, uncomfortable with the expression. Someone that close to death shouldn't look so calm. She should be fighting with every cell in her body to survive.

Why was she so passive?

Words from the *Bhagavad Gita*, the ancient Indian text vital to the Hindu tradition, drifted into my mind, as they often did.

Just as the dweller in this body passes through childhood, youth and old age, so at death he merely passes into another kind of body.

The crowd turned, and the Butcher's eyes flicked up, something off screen drawing his attention.

Dan sat forward, his elbow brushing mine as he rested it on his bent knee.

"That must be..." He didn't say her name. We both knew the story. Zerzan, our contact in the Peshmerga fighting force, had sent the video, and although it was barely twelve hours old, the rumors were spreading like wildfire on a dry and windy night.

The miracle woman took the city of Surama, then disappeared. Praise Allah. The prophet is showing her power to the world. The miracle woman is invincible. All women can rise up and change the world. Let the wolf out!

It was a very recent history playing out on the screen in front of us. It wasn't the only footage from the fall of Samara—an Isis stronghold in Syria—but Zerzan had said in her message that the footage was powerful. That it proved Sydney Rye was alive and working with the prophet.

The rumors of a miracle woman brought back to life by a female prophet—a messenger from God brought to earth to help women rise up against their male oppressors—started months earlier and had spread faster than anyone expected.

The CIA and other intelligence agencies were scrambling to deal with this new development, while my organization—Joyful Justice, an international vigilante network inspired by the vengeful acts of one young woman in New York City—was inundated with new requests.

The prophet claimed everyone decided their own value, and anyone who tried to stop a woman from expressing herself, living her life as a free and equal being, needed to be removed.

It was the kind of rhetoric that spawned new Butchers.

The crowd began to scramble, trying to escape the off-screen menace. The Butcher dropped his victim as an explosion sounded and dust and debris bloomed, instantly clouding a sunshine-filled day.

Through the veil of destruction, I just made out the Butcher leaping off the stage, his blade catching a reflection of flames before disappearing into the dust.

Another woman dressed in black robes, her blonde hair a tangled nest, climbed onto the stage and went to the fallen woman's side. Bent over the dying figure, the blonde head bobbed as her body shook. I recognize her from somewhere. She looked so damn familiar. Where had I seen her before?

"That's Sydney's mother, April Madden," Dan said, his voice low.

I glanced over at him, my lips parting in surprise.

Dan's green gaze stayed focused on the computer screen. The blue glow lit his skin, tan from his hours of surfing and running. He insisted that everyone exercised outdoors here. The island, the command center for Joyful Justice, was a former paranoid billionaire's escape plan. He had built an entire fortress inside an extinct volcano, then died of cancer before the world could implode and leave him safely cocooned on his own private island.

The fortress—with housing above ground level and the command center below, had enough room for a few hundred people. *Who did the billionaire plan to bring? What did his utopia look like?*

Joyful Justice bought the island from his estate several years ago. Was there something about this hunk of rock, in the middle of a wild, untamable ocean, that drew dreams like ours— visions of a safe world? But our dream was bigger than the billionaire's: we didn't want to save a few hundred people; we wanted to save everyone.

Everyone.

Dan found and purchased the island. Now, he was in charge of this headquarters of Joyful Justice, where all our missions were organized.

His team of experts worked ten stories underground, so Dan insisted that everyone spend at least an hour outside daily, working out, feeling the sun on their faces...remembering why they did what they did. What made life worth living.

Dan's sandy blond beard was streaked with the yellow of sunshine. His hair, grown out and still damp from a recent shower, was pushed back off his forehead. His brows were drawn together. "It's freaky how much they look alike. Like seeing thirty years into the future of Sydney," Dan said, his gaze riveted to the screen.

I turned back to the computer. Rye's mother, about Sydney's height and build but slower moving, not trained to kill like Sydney, held the dying woman in her arms, tears rolling down her cheeks. She glanced up at the camera for a moment, and those gray eyes—the color of sunlight blasting through a cloud cover to glint off a riled, windy sea—caught the lens for just a moment.

She wasn't afraid of death.

Just like the woman dying in her arms...but April looked like she wouldn't go down without a fight.

"Why is she there?" I asked. Dan shook his head, his lips pressed tight.

"We knew she was trying to find Sydney...I guess she did."

A hiccup of a laugh escaped me, and Dan turned, his heavy focus falling onto my smiling lips.

"What's so funny?" he asked. In my peripheral vision I saw the young woman go totally limp in April's arms.

I shook my head. "Nothing. Just." My eyebrows rose of their own accord. "It's not totally surprising that Sydney's mom can do whatever she wants."

Dan's mouth twitched into a small smile. "Must run in the family."

On screen, April released the young woman, laying a hand over her eyes to close them.

A black-clad figure, an Isis soldier, climbed onto the opposite side of the stage and aimed his weapon at April.

She turned to run and fell forward onto her hands and knees; her face, tear-streaked and coated with dust, was so close to the lens I could see small flakes of debris caught in her eyelashes.

My breath stopped. The soldier loomed behind her. *I was about to watch Sydney Rye's mother die.*

Blood exploded from the man's chest. He looked down at it, confused, before falling to his knees and tipping over, apparently dead.

April scrambled to her feet and looked around, trying to find the killer. No savior appeared. April's attention fell onto the Isis soldier's Kalashnikov, and she picked it up, her spine straightening and a smile pulling at her mouth. April Madden leapt off the stage into the chaotic crowd, disappearing off screen.

The camera caught the dust, fire, and smoke of war. The stage remained empty except for the young woman's body—deathly still in a world swirling with horror—every living person who passed the camera trying to avoid her fate.

The crowd shifted and all began to run in one direction, away from the square, away from where the Butcher had run. *Away from the Miracle Woman.*

A dog entered the frame, a giant mastiff, golden with a black muzzle and curled tail.

"I think they're called Kangals," Dan said.

He was flicking through his phone. Another dog appeared, a third, and then I saw Blue…Sydney Rye walking next to him. His head even with her waist, he was almost as broad as the mastiffs he moved with. Blue's nose tapped against Sydney's hip. She leapt onto the stage, the dog's circling around her—watching over her, but also herding her—as if she was a sheep, their charge.

Sydney bent down next to the body and felt for a pulse. Apparently finding none, she rose, and her head jerked toward the camera.

Those gray eyes pierced right through the lens, and I caught my breath, again. My hand shot out and grab Dan's forearm, squeezing.

Those eyes.

She looked desperate. Desperate to survive. Desperate to live. Willing to do anything. *She was feral.*

I recognized the look and the emotion behind it.

The scars on my body lit up as if fresh cigarettes were being ground into my flesh. Memories flashed; my muscle shook as I tightened the chain around my rapist's neck. Swallowing revulsion, I forced the sensations in my body to go away and sucked in a deep breath of Dan; ocean, sunscreen and warmed computer plastic.

Those men pushed me to where I could see Sydney was on the screen. They pushed me until I would do anything to escape, anything to survive.

And I did.

I fucking survived.

Sydney turned and jumped off the stage, the dogs following in her wake.

I looked down at my hand holding on to Dan and consciously unlocked my fingers, but his free hand came up and closed over mine, warm and calloused and comforting.

Tears sprung unwelcome to my eyes. Inhaling through my nostrils, I willed away the sting and quickly swiped my eyes with my free hand. There was work to do. Our mission was bigger than any one person. Certainly bigger than me. Bigger than what those men took from me.

Frustration squeezed my throat. *I didn't want them to have any power anymore. Would I ever be free?*

"I think we need to call the Joyful Justice council together," Dan said, referring to the governing body of our organization. His phone vibrated next to him, and I pulled my hand out from under his, freeing him to answer it. He looked at the screen. "It's Robert."

Dan's voice was a deep baritone when he answered, putting on a tough facade for Robert Maxim. That was a man to show no weakness to — he'd exploit it. He'd destroy us all, if it served him.

Dan's body tensed. "Sydney, where are you?"

"She's on the phone?"

He nodded and stood, pacing away.

I turned back to the screen, the video continued to play, showing an empty stage except for one dead body through a swirling mass of smoke —a hellscape.

But of course, Sydney Rye had survived.

She always did.

CHAPTER TWO
TROUBLE DEFINES ME

Sydney

"Dan?"

"Sydney, where are you?" It sounded like Dan...like a small piece of home.

My throat closed with unshed tears. "Mulberry is..." My hands sank into Blue's ruff, and he leaned against me. *Comforting.*

"Mulberry's what?" Dan's voice hardened, impatience roughening the edges.

"He's...I don't know..."

I looked around the room, the walls jittering and shaking in my vision.

"Where are you?" I heard Dan pacing, energy fizzing into his voice.

"I'm in a hospital. But. Is it possible?" I closed my eyes and tried to think clearly, but everything jumbled up on itself, tipping over into madness.

I'm crazy.

"We can send someone for you. Where are you?"

"Robert is here. He wants to take me back to the States—to Miami— so they can run tests."

"Where have you been?" His voice lowered to almost a whisper.

"I don't know, Dan." The battle flashed through my mind. And then the helicopter ride out of the city...we passed over a woman wearing a burka, surrounded by giant mastiffs. And she waved to me. *She saved me and then she controlled me.*

"Can you put Robert on the phone?" Dan asked, bringing me back to the room where I stood. "Sydney." Dan's voice dropped an octave. "Put Robert on the phone." *Like he wanted to talk to an adult.* My mother did the same thing when I was a kid and wanted to stay the night at a friend's house.

My mother. *Was she really here, too?*

"I think my mom is here. Why would my mom be here?"

"Okay, you need to put Robert on the phone."

"I'm not sure where he went." I looked around the empty room. Just me and Blue.

Dan took a deep breath. "Describe your surroundings to me." I heard him typing.

"I'm in an exam room...there is an exam table with paper on it. White walls. A sink. I'm seeing spots of light, and nothing is steady. The thunder and lightning are as bad as they've ever been." I closed my eyes, trying to escape, but found burst of color and strange shapes. "One minute I was dying and the next I found myself running down a mountainside toward a city...then suddenly I saw Mulberry falling..."

What was happening?

Fear tingled along my spine, releasing adrenaline into my system and making lightning crackle across the room. I blinked, trying to clear the bolts of electricity.

"Can you open the door, or are you a prisoner?"

"Not anymore. I don't think so."

But I had been...

I crossed to the door quickly, yanking it open. Robert stood on the other side, leaning against the wall, all casual, controlled power. He raised his eyebrows.

"Dan wants to talk to you." Robert nodded and stepped into the room, using his body to move me back. I stumbled, and his hand shot out, grabbing me by the elbow, steadying me. *Taking care of me.* He released me as soon as I had my footing and slipped the phone from my hand—*easy grace, easy control, slippery when wet.*

"Dan," Robert's voice came out deep and smooth—that still, chilled sea. I heard Dan's voice on the other side, like a duck squawking. Then Robert's response. "Mulberry's in surgery." Robert's gaze flicked to mine. "I don't have any more information than that on his condition. The doctor will come speak to us as soon as he can." Dan squawked some more. "They're not sure of Sydney's condition. She's hallucinating, has lost time; she has serious injuries, and some pretty impressive work was done on her in the field."

My hand reached to my side where scar tissue tingled under my touch. *I'd been shot and stabbed. That woman saved my life.*

Then held me prisoner.

More squawking from Dan. Robert looked away from me, his eyes scanning the room the way Blue scanned with his ears—like a predator who remained concerned about his safety.

Or maybe it was *my* safety.

"Yes, that's right; I want to take her back to Miami. I have specialists there—the same ones who worked on her right after the Datura poisoning."

Years earlier I'd been dosed with a highly potent and devastating hallucinogen. They called it the Devil's Breath in Colombia, and it was often used in robberies—extracted from the Datura plant, it sent your mind into a terrifying nightmare, leaving your body completely pliant. Victims emptied their bank accounts, escorted their burglars to their homes, and offered them their most precious possessions.

Blue killed the man who dosed me, but I'd stayed in a nightmare for almost a month—I'd finally woken up, but the hallucinations never fully left me. Thunder and lightning had plagued me ever since…but I knew they were hallucinations.

I knew what was real.

Robert held the phone out to me. Dan's voice came through, clear and familiar. "I'll have Merl meet you in Miami. I think Robert's right. We need to get you to a specialist."

"I can't leave." The truth fell from my lips. "I'm not done here."

"You need help, Sydney." Anger and frustration harshened his voice. Dan could never understand me. He could love me but never *get* me. My gaze traveled to Robert, his arms crossed, his lips set in a firm line—pure icy steel behind his eyes.

Robert was the only one who understood me.

"I have to..." What did I have to do? Why couldn't I leave this place? My gaze traveled to Blue. *He had puppies.* I couldn't leave without Blue's puppies.

But it was more than that. There was someone out there—someone who used me.

They'd saved my life and then controlled me.

If they could control me...they could control anyone. They were dangerous.

"I have something I need to do. Thanks for the concern. It's always good to hear your voice, Dan."

I hung up the phone before he could answer and handed it back to Robert. A smirk played on his lips. "What do you have to do?" he asked, his eyebrows raised.

"I have to kill the bitch that tried to use me."

His smirk slid into a sly grin.

"Let's go to Miami first, get you checked out. Then we can come back here and take care of everything." He moved in on me, entering my personal space.

"No. I'm not leaving."

"I can't protect you here, Sydney." Robert ground out the words, pulverizing them into almost a threat. *Almost.*

I bleed every month—death does not frighten me.

"You can't protect me anywhere, Robert. No one can."

A knock on the door interrupted us before Robert could respond. "Come in," he commanded, not taking his eyes off mine.

A man in blue scrubs entered the room. Robert turned, keeping me behind him. "Mr. Maxim." The doctor nodded his head in deference.

"How is he?"

This must be Mulberry's doctor.

I stepped out from behind Maxim, and the doctor's eyes drifted over me, before returning to Robert. *He guessed where the power lay.*

He guessed wrong.

"He's in critical condition. The surgery went as well as could be expected, but we're keeping him in a drug-induced coma."

"Will he recover?" Robert asked.

"He's lost his left leg just above the knee." A wave of revulsion ran over my body as I remembered Mulberry's bloody, torn flesh on the battlefield. "And he lost a lot of blood. I can't say what kind of mental capacity he will have if he wakes up."

"How bad are we talking about?" Robert's voice stayed neutral. Wind howled inside my head.

The doctor frowned. "It's possible he could be fine...or, in the worst case, left in a vegetative state."

"Can I see him?" I asked, stepping forward.

The doctor kept his gaze on Robert, who nodded slightly. "The nurse can show you to his room," the doctor said, stepping back and opening the door, speaking quietly to someone in the hall.

As I stepped out of the room—Blue on one side, Robert on the other—I grit my teeth, preparing myself for whatever would come.

Thunder and lightning and everything frightening brew inside you. Death cannot take you yet.

I stumbled as the woman's voice whistled on the wind of my madness...*She was real. And I had to find her.*

EK

April

My knees burned as I knelt on the hospital floor, eyes closed, palms pressed together. *Yes.*

I would earn a place by my daughter's side. We would change the world, *bring the word*...I was the mother of the miracle. Everything I did, I did for Joy.

Please provide me with the strength to follow her word, to follow the path you lay before me.

I will need strength. So much.

My lips formed words, prayers I knew by heart...they came straight from my heart, from the seat of my emotions, my direct connection to the Lord and Savior.

He chose me.

He chose Joy.

The doors of the waiting room squeaked, and I opened my eyes. Joy walked in, her dog with her, his big form pressed close to her side. Robert strode just behind her, almost an equal...but not quite.

He was speaking in a tone too low for me to hear, but my daughter did not look at him. Her eyes scanned the room and landed on me. They narrowed. I had a lot to atone for with my daughter: Joy, Sydney, the *Miracle Woman.*

Scrambling to my feet, I approached, my hands out in supplication.

She looked at my exposed palms with a dark gaze. "What are you doing here?" Icicles dripped off her voice. Robert turned to me, a small line of annoyance creasing his brow. He quickly smoothed his expression back into a calm mask of superiority. Here was a man who'd be shocked when he met our Lord...

"Joy, how are you? How is Mulberry?" I asked.

She shook her head. "You don't have a right to ask me anything."

"We are on the same side, Joy."

"No. We. Are. Not." The icicles' sharp tips stabbed with each word. *She hates me.*

Tears burned my eyes. "I'm so sorry, Joy; I never meant to hurt you."

"You can't hurt me." She stepped closer, and I forced myself not to shy away, to hold her gaze. *I love you.* "You are nothing to me."

"I'm your mother." *She couldn't mean it.* My little girl, that tow-headed toddler who came to my arms when she hurt her knee, when she needed comfort of any kind...*I made her.*

Her eyes held mine, the ice in her gaze freezing me as effectively as a winter storm. Then she turned and stalked away. Robert shrugged, his expression as cold and empty as ever, before turning to follow her. I grabbed his arm.

He looked down at my hand, black soot from the battle still staining the skin. "Let go," he said, his voice quiet, empty.

"Please, Robert, talk to her."

His eyes rose to mine. *So empty.* Another shiver passed over my skin. "I plan on talking to her, but I will not argue your case, April." He pulled free from me, and followed my daughter down the hall.

A huge, endless abyss opened inside of me. *Nothingness.*

A test?

Was God testing me? Yes, of course; this was all meant to be. *Everything was as it should be.* I had to prove to Joy that I was serious. I couldn't expect her to just *believe* me.

I'd hurt her. Pushed her and my son, James, away. Tears tried to cloud my vision, but I refused to be blinded by them. I had to continue to do the work. To pray. And the Lord would reveal my path.

I looked down at myself, at my bloody, ripped dress. Robert had taken my weapon—saying that I couldn't keep it and come to the hospital.

But I didn't have to stay here.

The elevator opened, and a nurse walked out, her head bent over a chart in her hands. I crossed the small waiting room and stepped into the empty elevator. A doctor got in next to me and pushed the button for the ground floor.

The elevator began to drop down. *Hell is beneath my feet but the Lord will lead me where I need to go.*

FK

Robert

I sat on the edge of the desk, the polished wood surface smooth against my rough canvas pants. The president of the hospital had offered me his private office for my calls.

I'd changed my clothing since the battle, but tension lingered in my muscles, and the taste of dust and death stained my tongue.

The phone rang, reaching across the ocean to Miami.

"Mr. Maxim, how can I help you?"

"Dale, good to hear your voice."

He cleared his throat. "I wish I could say the same."

A laugh bubbled inside me, but I didn't allow it to escape.

Dr. Dale Mitchell owed me. He owed me his life, his livelihood, *everything*.

I didn't find it difficult to own another person, to have him indebted to me, a debt so large he would never be able to repay it. I found it easy to control and command men like Dale.

It was the reverse...or an even playing field...that rubbed me the wrong way. I rarely did business or interacted with those that I could not control.

Except Sydney Rye.

Dr. Dale was a member of a very exclusive club that I founded. My sexual proclivities and his ran along similar veins. However, I had restraint. Whereas Dale... well, he had a problem. Or he did. *I solved it—saved him.*

He'd strangled a young woman. Killed her in his bed. In the bed he shared with his wife. That his daughter crawled into each morning for a cuddle.

I made the corpse in that bed go away.

I made sure that Dr. Dale stayed in practice, that his little girl still had a father, that his wife kept her husband.

And the victim...I arranged to give her an honorable death. Her family mourned a hero instead of a whore.

So Dale always answered when I called. When Sydney Rye was under the influence of Datura, he personally oversaw her care. And now he was going to fly to Turkey, had to get on the plane within 45 minutes, and help her again.

"Your flight leaves out of Opa-Locka Executive Airport."

There's was a pause, a moment for Dale to decide whether to argue. His daughter had a piano recital tonight. But he'd skip it. I let him have his moment, his pause.

"Is this about Sydney Rye?"

"Yes."

He cleared his throat. "Last we spoke, she'd recovered with only minor hallucinations…"

"They've become more severe."

"The storm?"

"Yes, thunder and lightning. And she lost time."

"How so?" Curiosity deepened his voice.

"She almost died, was taken prisoner. And doesn't remember much of it. And," I cleared my throat. "She was made to do things, against her will."

"Sexual?"

Sicko.

"No, but violent." *Starting a damn religion.* "We can discuss in more detail when you get here."

He grunted.

"You'll be able to help her." It wasn't a question. He *would* cure Sydney Rye or he would pay dearly. My fist tightened around the phone. *Someone had to pay.*

My next call was to Martha Emerson, a director at the CIA. We had a professional relationship. If she was a man, it would be an even playing field, but being seen as her sex alone kept her down, I didn't feel threatened by her. If anything, I liked Martha. I respected her.

She was smart, hardworking and loyal—I tried to hire her on more than one occasion, and she'd always turned me down. *A patriot.* But eventually, I knew I'd wear her down. In the meantime, she played nice, knowing that I held sway with the men she answered to.

"Robert." Her voice was clipped.

"Martha, how are you?"

I heard papers shuffling. "Why are you calling?"

"Checking in." I picked up a pen off the desk and twirled it over my fingers. "I have some information for you." *Pretend like you are giving a gift when really what you seek is an offering.* "Sydney Rye is alive."

The paper shuffling stopped. "She is?" Martha could not keep the eager tone out of her voice.

"Yes."

Martha cleared her throat. *She had to play this cool.* "We'd like to speak to her." *We.*

"What do you have on the prophet?" *I needed a name. An identity. Something to make her real.*

"We're working on it. Come in, bring Sydney, and we can discuss."

Nice try. "Give me what you have and then we can discuss Sydney..."

Martha sighed. *She wouldn't give me everything, but maybe it would be enough.* "We're pretty sure she is Syrian, trained in London. In her mid-thirties."

"Do you have a name?"

The papers shuffled again. "Bring Sydney in, and I'll give you the name."

"Martha, Martha, Martha. It's as if we've spent no time together."

"It's as if you're aiding and abetting a fugitive."

"Is she now?" I asked. "Last time I checked, Sydney Rye was the co-owner of Dog Fight Investigations, a U.S contractor...that can't look good. On paper, I mean." My voice dropped. "To have a wanted fugitive on the payroll. A radical."

"Where are you? I'll send transportation."

I laughed. "I don't need a taxi. Just a name."

"Come here and let's talk. Then I'll give you the name." *She didn't have a name.*

I had choices: let Martha talk to Sydney and hope that my connections could keep her free—and if not my connections, then threats of humiliation for the bureau. Or, keep Sydney hidden and take care of her myself. I needed to get Sydney medical care. *I could handle Martha.*

"I'm in Turkey, at Huzussu Medical Center—"

Martha cut me off. "Get out of there." Her voice was low and urgent. "I have very good intel an attack is going to happen there."

Shit. The CIA pulling strings, trying to control the Turkish government—the more unrest in Turkey, the more power the government could take, the more they could help the CIA. A terrorist attack at a private hospital would piss people off.

I hung up and yanked open the door of the office. The president of the hospital waited with his secretary, sitting on the edge of her desk, smiling down at her.

"Something bad is about to happen. I want Mulberry moved now."

He leapt into action, picking up the phone and beginning to bark orders. I checked my watch. *How long did I have?*

CHAPTER THREE
I WOKE WITHIN A DREAM

Mulberry

The door slammed, and my mother howled—a gut-wrenching, spine-tingling, hair-raising sound, like a banshee, a ghost...a woman scorned.

My father had walked out, leaving her for a younger woman.

"A whore!" My mother explained to her mother hours later as I sat in my grandparents' living room, the plastic covering the couch crinkling under me.

I stared at the familiar room, brown and tan carpeting that twisted over my toes when I was a child. Now, over a decade later, it had flattened under time and boots. My grandmother was always on my Papa's case about wearing his shoes in her house.

He sat in his recliner next to me. The Eagles played on the TV—men thrashing their bodies into each other, doing what men did best, battling in a field for glory.

Men did not make good domesticated creatures.

Papa, with his big belly, slumped shoulders, and sparse white hair clinging to his head, all that was left of his dark curly mane, sat slumped in the chair.

But my father was out there. He wasn't stuck at home. Like me. Like Papa. He was out saving lives and fucking whores.

My eyes wandered off the TV and up to the painting of Jesus that hung over the mantel. Cupped between his hands, the son of the Lord held his heart, circled in a crown of thorns, while his mournful eyes stared down into the fireplace. Which was filled with faux fall foliage and a carved pumpkin whose gap-toothed smile curled in with rot.

My mother's voice rose again. "How could he?"

My grandmother's soft response followed the exclamation. The sound of my mother crying drifted into the room, and Papa turned up the game.

"Second and goal late in the fourth quarter. If we score, we win."

I stared at Jesus's heart.

Dangerous to have it so exposed.

But, when you're the son of God, you probably don't worry about broken hearts.

Was my mother's heart broken? From where I'd sat, witnessing my parents' marriage, I'd think she'd be happy he'd finally left. They fought all the time. She hated him. And he didn't care about her—which is probably why she hated him.

He'd told me that he just didn't love her anymore. "But don't worry, son; I'll always love you."

I found that hard to believe. He must have said the same to her. That he'd always love her. It was in the marriage vows, wasn't it?

The Giants called a time out and the game broke for a commercial. My grandfather finished off his beer and glanced toward the kitchen, his mouth turning down into a frown. His gaze tracked to me. "Go grab me a brewski, will ya?"

Before I could answer, he shook his head and gave me a tight-lipped smile. "Never mind. I won't do that to you, Ralphie." He hauled himself out of the chair, his slippers, the same brown as the carpeting, slapping against his bare feet as he moved toward the kitchen. "In fact—" He looked over his shoulder at me. "It's high time you had a drink, boy."

He cleared his throat as he entered the kitchen. My eyes returned to the Jesus portrait. Mary had loved her son. She was a good mom. My mom was a good mom. Would my father's whore be a good mother to any children they had?

Would I be a good brother?

Papa returned with the beer and cracked the can open, handing it to me. The familiar scent reached my nose. "Your mother will be all right," Papa promised as he eased back into his recliner. "She's tough."

I nodded, taking a deep breath.

My father's words came back to me...right before he slammed the door. "She makes me happy, Mona!" *She makes me happy.* Was that how you got happy? A woman?

I sipped the beer, the bubbles tingling my nose, the bitter taste welcome. *This was not a child's drink. I was a man now.*

Papa returned his attention to the TV, after making sure I wasn't going to spit the beer everywhere. He let out a cheer as an Eagles runner plowed into the end zone.

I settled deeper against the plastic and tried to concentrate on the game, but the more of the beer I drank, the more my attention kept going to that heart in Jesus's hands. Was it throbbing? Beeping?

What was that sound?

The beer was going to my head. It was like I was swimming in place, like the room was wavering...

I finished the beer and put the empty can on the coffee table. The game ended, and Papa switched to the news, bringing me another beer. Darkness filled the windows, and Papa turned on the lamp next to his chair, throwing a yellow glow over the space.

My mother came out, her nose red and eyes swollen. "Let's go," she waved at me, sniffling.

I stood up, a little unsteady. Papa gave me a hug, his big softness enveloping me. He whispered in my ear. "You're the man of the house now; I expect you'll fill the role well, son."

"I will. I'll always love her." He squeezed me and then turned away. My grandmother fussed around my mother, hugging her then pushing us both out into the chilly night.

We walked back to our house in silence. As my mother unlocked the door, she paused and turned to me. Her green eyes held mine. She was beautiful, and my heart ached looking at her. She was so sad. My mom gave me a small smile. "I'll be okay."

"I know you will, Mom." I nodded. "You're very strong."

Her chin wobbled.

"I promise, Mom; I'll always be here for you." She burst into tears and pulled me close.

"You're a good man, son. I'm very proud of you."

She was heavy in my arms, the weight of her against me holding me in this place, in this world. My heartbeat rang in my ears, sounding almost like a beep.

EK

Sydney

The machines around Mulberry beeped, a high note above the thrumming of thunder in my brain. Each tone marked a heartbeat: one pump of that strong, fallible muscle.

Despite the pallor of his skin, the dark shadows under his eyes, and the way he laid there, so still—*deathly still*—Mulberry was alive. Still breathing, beating, being...

Curling my hand against his limp palm, lacing my fingers through his, I noted the clammy chill of his skin. Usually Mulberry was so warm...hot, even.

He was alive and yet appeared dead. I pushed him away and yet he followed me. He loved me and yet refused to save himself for me.

Everybody I love dies.

Tears stung my eyes, and I tried to blink them away, but they pooled hot and wet in my lashes then slid down my cheeks.

I'm so selfish.

If I was a better person, I never would've kissed him, never would've allowed myself those brief moments with Mulberry, the ones that set me free, that allowed me some form of obliteration.

My mind had been obliterated. The sizzling lightning in the corner of my gaze, the rolling thunder in the back of my mind, a patchwork of my memories, all pointed to a death of one kind. *I wasn't sane anymore.*

Had I ever been? I squeezed Mulberry's hand. He knew me before I was Sydney Rye. We met when I was Joy Humbolt, a mixed-up young woman in New York City whose life was upended when a dog she was walking sniffed out a body in an alley. Was I crazy back then, too? Was this destiny? Or had I chosen it all? Was it all my will that brought us here? Mulberry in a coma, his left leg ended above his knee.

The sheet showed the gentle outline of the stump. It looked almost like a party trick, a Halloween prank. When Mulberry did wake up—because he would wake up—he would find his life altered.

But he would adapt. He was strong and brave, and that beeping said he was still alive.

But his mind…

Your mind could change and yet the substance of you stay the same.

I held Mulberry's hand, searching for memories before I found myself running down that hillside into Surama…before I saw Mulberry fall.

I remembered that I was climbing, ready for death—sick of the lightning and thunder, of the storm I had built around myself. Sick of the violence and the deaths that thrived like strong winds in a low-pressure system.

I remembered fighting with a man who wanted me dead…my knife plunging home, the gurgled final breath of my victim. And then it all got real fuzzy. Real strange. The next memory is the battle in Surama, Mulberry lying in the street, war raging around us…Robert helping me get him to safety. The gap between those two sets of memories, Robert now tells me, was several months.

As we'd left Surama in Robert's helicopter, I'd seen a woman standing on the hillside, covered in a burka and long robes, surrounded by giant mastiffs. A part of me knew she was the one who'd saved me—performed surgery and kept me alive.

How she had held me captive and controlled me for so long, I didn't know. I felt a pulling at my mind, some kind of strange pressure—but it wasn't moving me. *I was in control again.*

I squeezed Mulberry's hand.

Fear had pushed me away from Mulberry—the fear of losing him. It didn't do any good; he teetered on the edge now. All my pushing had shoved him right into a battlefield—blown off his leg and left him in this hospital, the sheets tucked tightly around him, the machines beeping out the rhythm of his heart.

Blue leaned against my leg, and I used my free hand to pet his head.

"We have to go back," I said to Blue.

He sighed and rested his chin on my knee. I ran my finger up and down the length of his snout. He closed his eyes in appreciation.

"I have to kill her."

Why, though? Revenge? *She used me.* Told the world my recovery from near-death was a miracle—that my health, agility, my very existence was proof of God and His will.

I agreed that each of us decided our own value. Her message resonated inside me. I agreed with *Her* that women—any oppressed people—should rise up and fight against their oppressors.

But the thunder in the back of my mind told me she was dangerous. *Incredibly dangerous.*

Was there anything worse than a false prophet?

A false martyr?

My birth name, Joy Humbolt, sparked a vigilante network named Joyful Justice. One act of revenge and a story mistold changed the world.

I was sick of the lies.

This all had to stop.

My heart beat faster than the beeping at Mulberry's bedside. I couldn't keep living like this.

I refused to return to the United States, have some doctor tell me about my hallucinations. I knew what was real.

While under the spell of Datura, I was completely pliant. I'd watched the videos of myself: the way I nodded, the blank stare on my face. Robert Maxim, along with Dan and Mulberry, had kept me safe in a hospital room much fancier than this one. Robert Maxim held my hand, and I watched his lips move on the silent video. What did he say to me?

What did *she* say to me?

Faith is a weapon that I am willing to use.

It's the only thing more powerful than death.

You can wipe a civilization off the earth with a big enough bomb...or you can transform it into the civilization you want with the right faith. With a big enough lie.

I shuddered at the memory. I needed to confront this self-proclaimed prophet and understand what happened to me.

I needed to see Blue's puppies.

They were mine. Who was she to keep them from me?

I shook my head, trying to clear it of the harsh winds blowing against my ears. They were so loud the sound almost drowned out that steady beeping of Mulberry's heart.

The way that violence and greed for justice had almost blocked out the love he offered me. I pushed him away to save others, to save him.

Nothing I did ever worked. I needed to change. Needed a new approach.

I bent over Mulberry, pressing my cheek against the back of his hand. Breathing in the scents around me...trying to find the smell that was him.

But all that met me was the astringent sting of the hospital, the flowery perfume of clean sheets, and the iron-y tang of blood.

I couldn't stop Mulberry from dying. *I had no control.*

But I *could* go back to the woman who saved me. I would find her and those dogs and figure out what happened.

I couldn't do it alone.

Robert Maxim would help. He always helped me...because he wanted something from me.

My love.

A death sentence.

A distant crackle brought my head up as Blue straightened, his hackles rising. The building shook with the force of an impact.

Footsteps rang in the hall, and I dashed to the door. Through the small glass window I saw scrub-clad hospital workers running as smoke seeped into the air.

We were under attack.

I looked back at Mulberry. His bed was on wheels. A nurse ran to the door, and I stepped back as she pushed it open. She didn't glance at me as she yelled. "Get on the other side of his bed. We're evacuating. Move!"

I followed her orders, my hands wrapping around the cold metal of his bedside. She disconnected things, pulled plugs and threw wires across his chest. Mulberry didn't move.

The beeping stopped.

Because she'd unplugged the machine. He wasn't dead. He wasn't gone. *We were right here.*

Blue tapped my hip, reminding me that he was there, too, and as I began to push Mulberry's bed into the hall Blue stayed by my side.

My boots thudded on the linoleum floor, one of the wheels on Mulberry's bed squeaked, and Blue's nose tapped against my hip. My breath came even and strong despite a stinging pain in my side.

I was calmer now, in urgent motion, than I'd been sitting by Mulberry's bedside.

Mulberry's eyes remained closed even as his body shook with the movements of the bed.

The nurse's mahogany brown hair, pulled into a tight ponytail, danced behind her as she ran. Her face was set into tight lines of fierce determination as she navigated the hall.

The hospital had broken out into controlled chaos. People ran, but appeared to know what they were doing. The lights flickered, and dust fell from the ceiling as another impact shook the building. Our speed increased.

"He's top priority," the nurse yelled, pushing us past other waiting beds.

She opened a door and a hot, dusty wind blew in. I blinked against the grains of sand in the air. A helicopter, its blades twirling, prepared for takeoff. We pushed Mulberry to it, and with the help of another orderly, he was loaded in with two other patients.

The nurse pulled me back, her hand tight and strong on my bicep.

I was letting Mulberry go. Letting some strangers take him off into the air, trusting them to keep him safe because I knew that I couldn't.

Nothing could.

I stumbled back, Blue still tight to my side.

The nurse left us, and Blue and I watched the helicopter lift off the roof and fly away, the thwapping of its blades fading, allowing the roar of the fires below to reach us.

Smoke burned my eyes, and Blue urged me back into the building. I followed another orderly inside, my heart throbbing in my chest, adrenaline seeping into my veins. Making my way to the ground floor, I found front doors blown off their hinges, and smoke pouring into the lobby.

Blue directed me away from the exit, obviously sensing danger beyond, though I didn't exactly need a dog's instincts to know going out that front door might get me killed.

The smoke swirled, parting, and I saw Robert. He headed straight for me with a pistol in his hand and brow furrowed into a tight knot. When he grabbed my arm and began to pull me through the lobby toward another door, I let him lead me.

"Let's get to your ride," I said. "We've got to go find her."

A small laugh escaped him, but his stride didn't slow or shift.

"You'll help me find her," I told him. Knowing it was true. Knowing I could make Robert do whatever I wanted. *She wasn't the only one with power.*

He led me out a side door where a rusted, dust-covered Jeep waited. Robert nodded at the passenger side with his chin, releasing my arm. Blue and I climbed in, and Robert got behind the wheel. He placed his pistol between us, and I stared at it, my eyes traveling over the black matte handle to Robert's waist, where a knife was strapped.

He turned the Jeep on and put it in gear, speeding out of the narrow street. Reaching over, I unsheathed his knife, his eyes flicked off the road for a second.

"What are you doing?"

"Getting what I want. Take me to the prophet."

"I don't know where she is. Nobody does." Robert sounded annoyed. Not like I was threatening his life, more like I was trying to order a hamburger at a fish place.

"Take me to the cave where you saw me."

Robert's frown deepened, the memory of my rejection flitting across his face.

"Take me there or I'll kill you."

That brought a smile to his lip. "Will you kill me Sydney?"

"Don't try me, Robert."

He turned hard, and I fell against him, the knife scraping against the thick canvas of his black jacket. He reached over and tried to free it from my grip, but I was faster than him.

Despite the thunder and lightning, I was still fast. Still a goddamned killing machine.

We all decided our own value. We all had a right to our faith. But nobody used me. *Nobody.*

CHAPTER FOUR
FOLLOW THE FAITH

April

The church's steeple rose above the three-story houses that made up the majority of the buildings in this Turkish border city. I followed it and found myself in front of small, stone church with tiny stained-glass windows. I stumbled up the steps, my throat dry with thirst, my soul hungry for nourishment.

I pushed on the closed doors and found them locked. Banging my fists against the heavy wood, I heard my knocks echo inside. Muffled footsteps approached, and the door creaked open.

The scents of incense and wood polish filled my nose as my eyes closed. I fell forward, letting fate have me.

Strong hands caught my arms, holding me up. A man spoke in a language I didn't understand. He pulled me into the church and settled me into a pew, leaving the door open so that a shaft of sunlight illuminated the interior.

I bowed my head over clasped palms, thanking the Lord for bringing me here.

The man who'd helped me came into focus, kneeling next to me, his brown eyes wide with concern. I smiled at him. "Please, may I have some water?"

He nodded, his gaze scanning my face, down to my black robes that were stained with the dust and blood of battle. He hurried to close the door and then disappeared for a moment, returning with a glass of water.

I gulped it down and thanked him.

"You're American?" he asked in accented English.

"Yes, I am."

"What happened to you?"

I didn't know how to answer that. What had happened to me? When I learned of my daughter's disappearance in Isis-controlled territory I stole money from my husband, a preacher, and fled from Las Vegas to Istanbul, determined to follow my daughter, find her and make amends.

I almost died, but the Lord saved me and brought me into the path of women who I needed...and who needed me. Nadia, hardly an adult, yet stronger than any I'd ever know, flashed before my mind's eye—brows drawn together, eyes glittering with faith and power. *She died for what we believed in.* The Lord chose me to deliver the message of his prophet. That's why he left me alive.

"Did you get lost? The others are all here. They didn't mention they were missing anyone. Were you robbed?"

I cocked my head. *The others?*

"Where are they?" I asked.

"They're in the rectory. I will take to you to them, if you can stand. Are you injured?" His eyes ran over me again. "I can take you the hospital? There's one very close."

I shook my head. "No, I'm okay. I have been to the doctor. Please show me to the other Americans."

Taking my arm, he helped me down the aisle and through to the rectory, a humble living space where four women sat, tea cups on the coffee table between them.

While I didn't know them, I recognized them.

I'd seen women like them a million times. They attended my husband Bill's church. They felt the love of the Lord inside them and wanted to live in His light. I recognized the nervous movements of their hands, the knee-length skirts and silk blouses, the way their eyes widened as I entered the room.

The Lord brought me to them.

"Sisters," I said.

They stood up, confusion and fear warring on their faces. They wanted to be good Christians and help me, but they found my dress disturbing. The dust and blood terrified them.

They'd come here to save souls...not lives.

"Sisters, I'm here to join you."

"I'm sorry," one of them said, pulling out an iPad from her tote and looking at it. "I don't know who you are. Are you with the Ministry of Forgotten Souls?" Her accent was Southern, northern Florida maybe. Bill and I had done a lot of revivals in Florida.

"No, I'm not." I crossed the room quickly and captured the woman's free hand. She looked down at my cut and bruised fingers, at the burgundy polish still clinging to the edge of my nails.

"I've come from the battlefield. I bring a message."

"A message?" the woman asked, her eyes blinking rapidly.

My heart thumped in my chest. The words that came out of me were not my own, but a message from the divine spirit. "You decide your value."

The woman tried to step back, but I held onto her hand. "Have you heard of *Her*? Of the prophet?"

The woman turned and looked at her friends, "Now, I'm not sure what you're speaking of. But we're here to..."

I didn't let her finish. "You're here to help me. And I'm here to help you."

The minister stepped forward, taking my arm, trying to pull me back. "I think you need a doctor."

I turned to him and lay my hand on his forearm, my gaze holding his. "I don't need a doctor, young man. But thank you for your kindness."

"Wait," the woman whose hand I held spoke, narrowing her eyes at me. "I recognize you. You're...aren't you April Madden?"

I smiled. "Yes, I am."

"You're Bill Madden's wife." She looked past me to her friends. "She's from Bill Madden's ministry. How did you get here?"

I smiled. "I have a story to tell..."

EK

Anita

The Joyful Justice Council gathered.

Dan sat next to me in front of a bank of computer screens.

Merl called in from Joyful Justice's training center in Costa Rica, his long black hair pulled back into a tight bun, brown eyes sharp and focused despite the late hour there. A martial arts master and dog trainer, Merl owned three Doberman pinschers and could kill almost anyone with his bare hands. His calm demeanor and steady leadership made him a vital member of the Joyful Justice Council.

Lenox Gold, originally from Senegal, was smart and ruthless but also compassionate...he was like that old cliché, a hooker with a heart of gold. The man made a fortune selling the bodies of other men to desperate, hungry women and then turned around and used that money to protect the people he sold, and to protect those who didn't want to be sold. He lounged in a beige chair, his dark skin glowing under the pale blue light cast from his computer screen. I didn't know where he was... didn't need to.

While Sydney was a member of the council, we'd decided to proceed without her. Dan had tried Robert's phone, but it went straight to voicemail...besides, Sydney was in bad shape and was more than likely compromised in some fashion by her time in captivity.

The three men on the council all waited for me to speak. Everyone had seen the video of the battle and the question that floated in the air was what we should do about it...if anything. As Joyful Justice's public relations and marketing head, it was up to me to advise the rest of the council on our next steps, but it would be our mutual decision.

"As you all know, the *I am Her* video has been translated into 25 languages and viewed 90 million times."

The video, featuring the self-proclaimed prophet wearing a burka and disguising her voice, explained God sent a message through her: each person's value was their own to decide. It had gone viral in a way that only a few such inspirational videos ever have.

It had far more views than any Isis recruiting video. More even than some guy getting hit in the balls by his kid's baseball bat. The prophet's eloquent call that we all "let the wolf out" had more views than any video ever produced by Joyful Justice.

"From what I understand, the prophet doesn't have access to this new video of the Syrian battle. It is just Zerzan and us. Isis actually made it. They've used footage like this in other propaganda films." The rest of the council nodded...they'd seen the Butcher at work. "Zerzan could obviously release it on her own, but she wants to follow our lead on this. We don't know what—if any—influence the prophet may have with the Peshmerga guerrillas...so she may still get her hands on it."

In the months since the prophet's video's release, her message had spread quickly through Isis territory and the Middle East, where women were rising up and murdering the men who controlled them—often their fathers, brothers, or husbands.

It was brutal.

Lenox nodded slowly, his eyes trained on me. I cleared my throat.

"Her statements obviously align with those of Joyful Justice: the value of all people; the equality of women; the call to rise up against those who hurt or oppress you."

All the men nodded, but no one spoke.

"But, claiming that God has somehow ordained all this..."

I looked down at my hands for a moment. There were scars on my fingers, faded but still there from the cuts I sustained during my captivity.

Did it matter why people rose up, as long as they did?

"We've steered clear of religion until this point, allowing each member to follow their own faith—or whatever else motivated them. This would be pushing a specifically religious message. I've only had a couple hours to think about it." I chewed on my lip for a moment. "And while I know that we can get a lot of traction with this video—it's bloody, it's frightening, it's vivid..." I looked over at Dan. He was watching me with those green eyes of his, all his focus leveled on me. "I know this video could help our cause, but I think it could also destroy it."

Dan nodded slowly. "My thinking on this isn't completely clear either." He looked at Merl. "And therefore I believe we should hold off on making a decision for at least a few more hours. Take some more time to let it sink in."

"But we will have to get Zerzan an answer soon," Merl said.

"Yes." I nodded.

Lenox spoke, his accent lyrical and beautiful. "This is very powerful stuff. Sydney looks like an avenging angel—one that was miraculously brought back from the dead." He shifted in his chair, leaning closer to the screen. "I'm not saying we should release it. Not yet, as none of us are clear what to do." He gave a small, almost apologetic smile. "We've tried to contain the zealotry that is inherent in an organization like ours. We think we are right to do so."

"We are right," I interrupted, not able to stop myself.

Lenox nodded, leaning back into his chair. "Of course, Anita, I agree."

The way he said my name sent a shiver down my spine. The man was pure magnetism. "But, being so sure can lead to blindness," I went on. He was nodding, and I felt myself nodding with him. "We must be very careful."

Merl leaned closer to his screen. "I agree. Releasing this without thinking about it deeply would be a mistake. We don't want to be rash. And I'd like to hear what Sydney has to say. It's her image up there." He tilted his chin. "It's possible she doesn't want this out there."

I gritted my teeth, and Dan spoke my thoughts for me.

"Obviously, Merl, this is bigger than Sydney. What she wants is a consideration, but it certainly is not *the* deciding factor."

Merl frowned. "Since when is what a person wants done with their own image not a deciding factor for us? Releasing this tape will put her face everywhere. Everything I know about Sydney tells me that she likes to stay hidden. She doesn't want people knowing what she looks like."

"It's too late for that," I said.

"Is it?" Merl asked.

"She's already being treated like a martyr," Dan pointed out. "Zerzan's troops have her picture on their playing cards."

"They have *Joy's* picture." Merl referenced Sydney's birth name. Joy Humbolt avenged her brother's death, killing a powerful man that the law couldn't touch. Her act of bravery, of vengeance, spawned Joyful Justice. But Sydney hated to talk about it—she was a woman of action, not of stories.

Merl leaned in toward the camera. "Sydney Rye, the miracle woman." His brows rose. "*She* hasn't been exposed. I want to talk to Sydney before I vote to do it."

"Well," Lenox spoke up. "We may have different reasons for agreeing, but we all do agree that we should wait." He shrugged. "If Zerzan decides to release it, or the prophet somehow gets a hold of it, then it's out of our control. And we can react to that when the time comes." He held my gaze. "I'm sure Anita will be prepared. She always is."

I nodded, acknowledging the compliment.

"Until that time," Lenox continued, "I'll arrange to fly to Turkey to be with Sydney and Mulberry. I'm not far now and we will need a team member by Mulberry's side to arrange care during his recovery."

"I agree with Lenox." I closed my eyes for a moment, organizing my thoughts. "The thing is that I think things are changing. Quite drastically. The message of *her*, the wolf inside all women, all of this is moving faster than anything I've ever seen. #IAmHer is trending higher on Twitter every single day. It's been covered by CNN, the BBC and other major news networks. We are going to have to face it eventually."

Lenox nodded. "I hear you. I will think deeply about this."

"Yes," Merl said. "Let's talk again soon." He looked at his watch, and I saw the scars on his wrists. They were thick and pink, still new yet no longer raw. *Sydney saved his life, too.*

Merl knew what it was to be a prisoner. But his body had not been violated.

Rape was a weapon in war. A weapon that was being used in the Middle East, by Isis, and in Africa by Boko Haram…and in other countries all over the world. It was the oldest weapon. And this prophet was the first person claiming to be a voice from God whose central message was female resistance to all forms of exploitation.

Why hadn't such a prophet stepped forward sooner?

Because she wasn't from God? God was always depicted as a man—he created Adam in his image and then the devil convinced Eve to eat an apple and women ruined paradise…

Women were the problem. In almost every religion women were the fucking problem.

Even in the *Bhagavad Gita*, which my father read to me and I still studied, quotes from it often seeming so true to my life. Even in that sacred text that I loved, women were dangerous, on the verge of sin at any moment if given freedom.

When irreligion is prominent in the family, O Kṛṣṇa, the women of the family become polluted, and from the degradation of womanhood, O descendant of Vṛṣṇi, comes unwanted progeny.

This Her Prophet offered an answer, a solution: let women decide their own value, and rise up against any who try to stop them. A thrill ran through me, raising goosebumps…the places this could lead…the ways it could change the world, if enough people believed.

"I just want to say one more thing." All eyes turned to me. "I think it's possible this prophet thinks she's hearing God's voice, but it could also be a trick. The fact is that any secular argument about why women are equal is not going to be as powerful as one handed down from the Almighty Lord."

Dan nodded next to me. "I agree." The other men mumbled their agreements.

"Let's keep that in mind. If our goal is to help people rise up against their oppressors then having God on our side might not hurt," I continued.

"Unless it's the devil," Lenox said.

"Excuse me?"

"They say the best trick the devil ever played was convincing man that he did not exist. What if the best trick was convincing Man that he was God?"

"They probably should have checked with some women." My voice came out harsh. Only the devil would think women were equal? Says one of three men on a council with only one woman currently active. And these were the *enlightened* men of the world.

I wanted to bang my head against the desk, but I firmed my jaw instead. When Lenox Gold took over Malina's place on the council, I'd agreed because he had the expertise we needed. Lenox and Malina were good friends and moved in the same world.

But when Sydney went missing, it left me as the only female voice.

"All I'm saying is that we must be careful who we align ourselves with," Lenox said, his brows conferring, his eyes watching me. "This prophet could change her message at any time. By aligning ourselves with this preacher in a burka, we could turn off people of other religions. As you said earlier, we've remained out of religious debate, which allows people of all beliefs, including atheists, to seek our help."

"Yes, I know that. I'm just saying that people shouldn't have to give up their faith in God to believe that women are equal."

He held my gaze, his honey brown eyes soft. "I understand that, Anita. I certainly haven't given up my faith. And I know that women are equal to me. Many of them are better." He smiled slightly, his chin dipping, as if to indicate that I was one of those better women.

We said our goodbyes, agreeing to convene again soon, and then disconnected. Dan stood up and stretched, reaching his fingers toward the ceiling, his T-shirt rising up and exposing the waist of his jeans, a line of tan skin and a trickle of blond hair.

I looked back down at my scarred hands.

"Want to grab a bite?" Dan asked.

I shook my head. "I think I'll work for a while longer." Looking up at him, I forced a smile.

He left the office, and I sat in the silence, just listening to my own breath.

Religion gives us power and takes it away.

But which was this?

CHAPTER FIVE
FRIEND OR FOE

Robert

I consciously unclenched my hands from the wheel of the Jeep. Sydney Rye sat in the passenger seat, my knife still in her grip. *Fuck, I liked it when she threatened me.*

Blue sat at Sydney's feet, his ears perked forward and eyes on the road ahead. I'd gotten Mulberry onto a helicopter, and he was headed to Istanbul where I'd arranged for his care to continue at the best hospital in the city. *I did it all for her.* And she'd thanked me by threatening to cut me open...

Still, I'd helped her leave the city, and now the open road lay before us.

Sydney petted Blue's head, her eyes tracking the sparse traffic around us. She wanted to go to where I'd encountered her under the prophet's control. Sydney's silent dismissal at that time had felt like a blow to the chest.

My ego forced me to turn away from her—*I should have chased her down and made her look into my eyes.*

Should I take Sydney to that cave now? The chances of the prophet being there were slim to none, unless the woman was a total fool, which, judging from her actions so far, she wasn't.

This prophet was a skilled surgeon and savvy marketer.

The work she'd performed on Sydney narrowed down our list of suspects. There were only so many surgeons in the region who could perform the work done on Sydney, let alone not in an OR. And most of them were presumably male.

It was thus only a matter of time before we figured out the woman's identity. Before we hunted her down, before she fell under *my* control.

"How far is it?" Sydney asked.

"Far," I answered, keeping my voice steady. "We have to fly...into dangerous, contested territory."

I had to consciously unclench my hands again. Every cell in my body wanted to protect Sydney. Wanted to trick her, sneak her back to Miami, and get her the care she needed.

Could I convince her to wait for Dale to arrive?

"Look, I'll make you a deal." I felt Sydney's gaze land on me. *She didn't trust me.* "Let me take you to Istanbul, to the same hospital Mulberry will be at. You could be with him." *Dangle the carrot.* "Your doctor is on his way from Miami to check you out. We can make sure you are not on the verge of having an aneurysm or something similarly awful before we go back to find her."

Silence stretched so long that I turned to look at her. Sydney's gaze had dropped to Blue. She played with one of his ears as he continued to stare out the front window.

"I'm not going to have an aneurysm, Robert."

"You've no idea." I bit off my words. Anger welled in me, and I battled it, wrestling the rage into calm, into control. Anger didn't work with Sydney Rye. *Nothing did.* She turned to look at me—those silver-gray eyes so strange, so unique, so intelligent. *So brave.* "I don't want you to die." The words left me with a sigh. A prayer. *Stay with me.*

A small smile curled the edges of her lips. "Don't worry, Robert. I don't want to die either. Anymore. But I do need to find her. I do need to stop her."

"Sydney, you can't stop what's already begun. You can't turn back time."

"I'm not trying to turn back time, Robert. I'm just trying to make it right."

My hands tightened on the steering wheel and I couldn't relax them. "Make it right? There is no such thing. Don't you get that yet? There is no making anything right. Everything is wrong and always has been. And always will be."

I took a left, headed toward a place I knew we could land a helicopter —to get us lifted close to the cave, though it would still be a long hike. I was doing what she wanted me to...only Sydney could get me to do what she wanted.

Dammit.

"You're wrong, Robert. Things can be right."

She said it like she believed it, like a Christian tells you that Jesus is the son of God, or a Muslim tells you Muhammad spoke the word of God, or an atheist tells you it's all a lie.

Sydney Rye believed in right and wrong. She believed in black and white. You'd think the gray of her gaze might give her some hint at the subtle shades of morality.

"Fine," I swallowed, rolling my shoulders. "I'll take you to the cave. She won't be there." *But we'd be alone, in the wild, together.*

"Thank you." The quiet of her voice startled me. I took my eyes off the road to stare at her. She was looking right back at me, her gaze sharp and focused. The scars around her left eye, made by her brother's murderer—from the first battle she ever faced—were faded now but still pulled at her sensitive flesh, the subtle flaws making her more beautiful.

"You're welcome," I said.

She nodded. "You've done a lot for me, Robert. I do appreciate it." I turned back to the road, feeling a lump in my throat—a sensation that didn't make any damn sense and was completely unacceptable.

"You saved my life; I want you to know that I know that."

All I could do was nod. She had me by the heart; she had me by the balls. Sydney Rye had me. And I'd never be free.

EK

Sydney

Robert pulled up in front of a gate. The wall on either side stretched as far as I could see and was topped with barbed wire.

He spoke into a voice box by the entrance. "It's Robert Maxim." The gate opened.

"A friend of yours?" I asked.

"Someone who owes me a debt. Be prepared, he might try to kill us."

I looked over at him, expecting a smile or something. But his mouth was a determined line. "You're serious?"

"Yes, this is the fastest way to get out. Deacon can meet us with the helicopter. But we might be walking into a trap."

"And you waited till now to tell me?"

"What would you have done with more time to prepare?" That smile showed up.

"You can be such an ass," I said, pulling my pistol.

Robert placed his hand on top of mine, his thumb running the length of my index finger. "Keep your weapons hidden. If he does decide to kill us, it won't be obvious. He would be foolish to take me head-on. He knows I have...protocols in place." *Protocols?* Of course he did. Robert Maxim didn't walk into a vipers' nest without the antidotes to viper poison. "Can I have my knife back?"

I looked down at the shiny blade, catching my reflection: red-rimmed eyes, and a frown pulling at my lips...the same way my scars pulled at my skin. I passed the weapon to Robert, and he slipped it back into its holster.

The driveway wound through manicured landscaping. The grass was an unnatural green for this desert area, and the elegantly placed trees shone with health and irrigation.

The house came into view, a giant stone edifice. Three stories high, with tall windows, it looked like a French château that belonged on the outskirts of Paris, not on the border between Syria and Turkey.

"What is this place?"

"His wife makes the decorating choices," Robert said. There was something in his voice. "And she is particular."

"His wife?"

Robert nodded. "She used to be my wife."

I laughed. "This guy is married to your ex-wife?"

"Yes. Angie, my first wife."

"She's got great taste in men. Almost as good as her architectural ideas." I laughed again, my side hurting.

"Angie is a beautiful woman."

"I'm sure she is."

A beautiful woman. He meant on the outside. That's where her value lay. In her hot ass, her high cheekbones, a set of glittering eyes and probably a rack as robust as her decorative hedges.

Robert had been married three times. I'd met his third wife in New York. Pammy. A high-end stripper turned mistress turned wife.

I'd never understood how he'd gone through three wives. Robert, so cold, so calculating. Why would he marry and divorce three different women?

"Why do you marry them?" I asked him.

"A wife can't be forced to testify against her husband." He paused. "Besides." A small smile stole over his lips. "I'm a traditionalist. I like marriage." He looked over at me as we pulled up to the entrance of the château.

"You like marriage? That's why you do it so often?"

"Yes," he answered with a tone in his voice I couldn't quite interpret.

He asked me to marry him once. I saw the proposal for what it was: an attempt to control me.

But I wasn't like his other wives...Pammy must have been easy enough to control with cash. Maybe he enjoyed the emotional games. Wanted to own a woman's heart, not just her ass.

Robert shifted, and I saw him adjusting his pistol. "You ready?" He raised his eyebrows.

I shrugged, a streak of lightning shooting across my vision. "Sure."

A butler came down the stone steps and opened Robert's door. I went to open my own, and Robert shot me a look. I shot one back and climbed out of the vehicle.

The butler's eyebrows rose when he saw me. I guess I wasn't the kind of woman Robert Maxim usually traveled with.

I had fresh, clean clothing on, and my hair had been washed and neatly tucked under a billed cap... so it's not like I was dripping in blood and brandishing a knife, but the way the butler looked at me, you'd think I was.

Maybe it was Blue? The butler was eyeing him like he was a tiger.

"Hello, Guc," Robert said to the Butler. "Hope you're doing well."

The man recovered, swallowed and nodded. "Always a pleasure to see you, Mr. Maxim. I hope you'll be staying with us."

His eyes ran over the Jeep, looking for bags.

"Not today; we have a helicopter picking us up. Just wanted to stop by and see Mr. and Mrs. Kilicli."

Guc nodded. I came around the car, and Robert offered me his arm. I looked at it for a moment, and he raised his brows at me, communicating *I'm giving you what you want, play the fuck along.*

I wrapped my arm through his, and with Blue close to my hip we moved up the stone steps, Guc leading the way.

The entryway was tiled in black and white. A fountain tinkled, and a chandelier above us glowed with sunlight that poured through the glass ceiling.

A woman's laughter reached us, followed by a man's soft murmur.

Robert and I waited in the hall while Guc went ahead and opened a library door. He spoke quietly with the occupants and then returned to usher us in. He bowed as we passed through.

We entered a gigantic room, its floor-to-ceiling windows looking out onto a manicured garden behind the house. Couches and chairs were grouped in intimate seating areas. On one couch, a man and woman sat close to each other, her hand in his as she smiled up at him.

With skin the color of café mocha, glowing and unlined, shiny black hair cascading down her back, and eyes the bright gold of wheat under the blush of a setting sun—Robert Maxim's first wife stole my breath with her beauty. How could someone this young-looking be on her second marriage? Maybe people didn't age the same when they lived in faux chateaus. And had butlers.

She blinked, thick black lashes caressing her high cheekbones. Her ruby lips spread into a wide and inviting smile then quickly tempered themselves, forming into something smaller, sultrier. She nodded at Robert as her husband stood.

Shorter than me but far broader, the man who approached us was mustachioed and bald, wearing a tailored suit. He walked like he owned a faux chateau and laughed as he crossed the room, holding out a hand. "Robert Maxim. I thought I'd never get you back here again. Not after last time." He laughed harder.

"When a man steals your wife, it's hard to return to his home." Robert shook the man's hand. I suppressed a smile.

"Allow me to introduce my business partner, Sydney Rye. Sydney, this is Mustafa Kilicli and Angie."

Angie followed in the wake of her husband, her long dress swiping behind her like a tail. She extended her hand to me. I looked at my own, making sure that it wasn't smudged with dirt or blood before extending it to her. Angie's soft and elegant palm met my calloused one—her hand looked like a trapped bird within the predatory grip of my fingers.

"Pleasure to meet you," she said, her accent impossible to nail down. She could've been from anywhere...anywhere sexy and cosmopolitan, that is.

"Come, we were just about to have lunch."

"We can't stay," Robert said. "I appreciate the hospitality but we have a helicopter arriving soon." His eyes darted out to the expansive lawn beyond the gardens. "Unfortunately, we are in a hurry."

"Don't be silly, you must join us," Mustafa said, slapping Robert on the back. A low, almost inaudible growl left Blue's chest. Angie's eyes darted down to him. "What a beautiful dog. I keep Afghans."

I smiled at her. "How nice for you."

She nodded; it was nice for her.

Angie leaned forward and kissed Robert on the cheek. Did she linger? I couldn't tell. Mustafa's frown, the way his fists clenched and the color that stole over his cheeks, seemed to say she did.

He wanted Robert Maxim dead.

But did he have the balls to try and kill him?

I guessed we'd find out soon enough.

CHAPTER SIX
ONE HELL OF A LUNCH

Sydney

A long table draped in a fine white tablecloth, with multiple glasses, forks, spoons and knives at each setting, dominated the dining room.

My stomach rumbled at the smells emanating from the nearby kitchen. Blue pushed his nose into my hand—we were both hungry.

It would probably be inappropriate to feed him from the table here. Not that I'm Miss Manners or anything, but I didn't want to insult our hosts; after all, they already wanted to murder Robert Maxim.

Robert pulled out a chair for me, and I sat. His fingers trailed over my shoulders as he stepped away, sending splinters of lightning spidering across my vision.

Blue moved under the table and rested his chin on the toe of my boot.

Mustafa pulled out Angie's seat across from me. Between us a silver candelabra shone in the sunshine that poured through the wall of windows behind her. As Angie sat, she flipped her long hair over her shoulder; it splayed out in an arc reminiscent of a shampoo commercial.

The butler reappeared, and Angie nodded at him. He turned around and left through the door he had come in.

A moment later a uniformed maid entered. Round and soft, her face lined with age and hard work, she appeared to be in her fifties. The huffing of her breath and rosy cheeks made the maid seem friendly—hardly like a poisoner.

No one else looked at the woman as she placed a covered serving dish down near Angie. Our hostess continued to chat with Mustafa and Robert about God only knows what. They all acted as if there wasn't a fifth person in the room.

She was real, though. Not like the thunder that blotted out the conversation twittering around me.

The maid left, taking the silver top of the serving dish with her, and Angie's eyes glided over to the platter of poached salmon displayed on a bed of lettuce.

Robert followed her gaze, and his expression twitched for just a moment.

"Your favorite," Angie said, leaning over to serve Robert a slice of the salmon with a perfectly browned lemon on top.

Robert nodded, not commenting on her intimate knowledge of his preferences.

Angie glanced at me. "Have you and Robert known each other long?" She smiled softly, but her gaze was sharp. Angie wasn't a fool. Pammy hadn't been either.

Robert was attracted to intelligent women who knew how to use their sexuality to gain themselves power. And then he enjoyed taking that power from them.

"A few years," I answered. Angie nodded, standing slightly to place a slice of salmon on my plate. "But I'm not aware of his food preferences," I smiled at Angie. *I'm not fucking him.*

Robert cleared his throat. "Are you enjoying it here, Angie? Last time we spoke the summers were a little hot for you." Mustafa's brow furrowed. Was it a revelation that Angie and Robert spoke?

"That was over a year ago," Angie said with a smile. "We've had new air conditioners installed. And the indoor pool is finished. Also, we've air conditioned the riding ring, so my equestrian pursuits don't have to stop in any season."

"Weren't the rains a bit much for you?" Robert asked, cocking his head, as if he was genuinely curious and not just trying to fuck with her.

But I knew what he was doing. Angie had tried to put a wedge between us, to remind me that she knew him better. But all she had managed to do was make Robert expose her—expose the trust she continued to share in him to Mustafa, whose face was now turning a disturbing shade of purple.

Was Robert trying to get himself killed? Did he need control so badly he was willing to risk his life to claim it?

I'm not the only insane person at this table.

Angie turned away from him, finished serving the salmon, and then began to pour the wine.

"Your home is beautiful," I said, filling the tense silence that had settled over the room. Robert picked up his wine and muffled his laugh into it.

Mustafa's gaze remained locked on his wife. His eyes were sparkling black—the Atlantic ocean on a cloud-covered night. But when Angie turned to him and laid her hand on his thigh, they softened—the Caribbean at midnight, before the moon has risen with the stars glowing brightly above.

"Thank you," she said, acknowledging my compliment but keeping her attention on her husband. "Mustafa is so good to me," her lips parted in a small, private smile just for him. "He let me design it myself."

"That's wonderful," I said, my voice almost drowned out by a sudden rumble of thunder. "It must be wonderful to have a husband you love so much."

Mustafa's dark eyes turned to me. They were questioning and sharp. *Did I know something he didn't?* No way, buddy. In fact, there's a storm cloud dancing over your head in my vision.

The maid returned with another platter, this one with asparagus and wild rice.

"Magda makes the most delicious salmon," Angie said.

"Has she been your cook long?" Robert asked.

Angie began to serve the asparagus. "Just this season. I found her in

Paris. You won't believe what we have to pay her to keep her here." She laughed, the sound like crystal glasses clinking.

"Anything for my love," Mustafa said, his voice a deep rumble as his eyes latched onto his wife.

He loved her. But he didn't trust her. It must be almost impossible to trust a woman as beautiful as Angie if you were a man as rich as Mustafa.

None of us had touched our food but as Angie piled the last spoonful of wild rice onto her own plate she gestured to Robert. "Please, eat."

Robert smiled. "Ladies first, of course."

Angie shook her head, smiling, and began to eat her salmon. Mustafa followed suit and my mouth watered at the delectable meal in front of me but I wasn't about to feed it to myself or Blue without making sure those two didn't drop dead first.

Robert went to put down his glass of wine and spilled it over his plate. Jumping up with a cry, he knocked my plate off the table. "Shit, sorry," Robert said.

Blue sniffed the salmon that landed by my boot, but didn't eat it.

Was it poisonous? Or was he just anti-lemon?

"We'll get Magda to get you another plate," Angie said, reaching for a bell next to her glass.

"Thank you," Robert said. "Oh, but look, Sydney, I've spilled all over your pants."

I looked down at the black canvas pants and saw a few spots of wine.

"Oh, I can give you something to wear," Angie said immediately, her eyes widening. *She wanted to dress me up like a doll.*

Or get me alone to try and kill me?

"I think it's probably—"

Robert cut me off. "That's so kind of you, Angie, thank you. Sydney..." He raised his eyebrows, turning to me.

Perhaps he wanted alone time with Mustafa. I was still hungry, though. *Dammit.*

Maybe I could bribe Magda into giving me some food that wasn't poisoned before we got out of here.

I'd had a bowl of lentil soup at the hospital, but it was fully digested by now, and I was starving—having food placed in front of me and then rudely taken away by an on-purpose-accidental wine spill and the possibility of death sucked.

Angie was already up from the table and headed toward the hall. She beckoned to me. Blue came out from under the table as I stood. When I reached her, Angie linked her arm through mine, and her elbow brushed the gun under my jacket. Her eyes flickered for a moment, but she didn't say anything.

She must have known I was armed. Dressed the way I was, traveling with Robert Maxim, here for a helicopter pick-up. *She wasn't stupid.*

She might be armed, too. I wouldn't be surprised if there was a knife in her garter, even a small pistol. I kind of wanted to see it.

However, I didn't want to borrow her clothing. My canvas pants, T-shirt and jacket were the perfect thing to be wearing right now. But if she was going to dress me up, Robert must have his reasons for it.

As she escorted me through the house, a storm cloud followed us, and I felt that lure, the magnetism of *Her* pulling at me. Hopefully we'd get to the prophet before she got back into me.

EK

Robert

Angie and Sydney left, their arms linked. An odd pair—one all dark sexuality, the other fair and pure grit.

"You have strange taste in women," Mustafa said before shoveling a bite of salmon into his mouth.

"Eclectic," I corrected him, filling my wine glass with water. He snorted. "I appreciate you allowing me use of your lawn." I gestured to the windows behind him.

Mustafa sat back, keeping his fork in his fist. "You know the only reason I do so is for Angie. She is my life."

I nodded and sipped the water.

Mustafa wanted me dead. I'd guessed it before we arrived, but when Angie greeted me with a kiss, I saw the intent on his face.

One of us would die today.

It wouldn't be me.

"You're the one who stole my wife so..." I shrugged.

Mustafa frowned deeply. "She's my wife."

"Yes, I know that, Mustafa. But she *was* mine when you met her."

I'd brought Angie with me on a business trip—Mustafa sold weapons, and we'd worked together for over a decade when I introduced the two. I'd guessed that he'd fall for her, most men did. And I needed to get rid of her. She was on the verge of leaving me; just needed a soft landing.

I'd hoped it would give Mustafa a sense of guilt, that he'd feel indebted to me. When you steal a man's wife you do owe him something...Mustafa didn't agree.

Angie suffered terrible guilt about leaving me. *Or so she claimed.* But she left me because I was a cold, hard, and unforgiving husband who wanted to control everything about her. Angie ran to Mustafa because he gave her everything she wanted. Of course, he still controlled her. Men like us always held the power...but I'd never let Angie stick me in a chateau. All the curlicues and flourishes, all the rounded edges. I preferred cold, hard glass and polished metal.

An image of Angie strapped to a table, at my mercy, rose into my mind. What a wonderful honeymoon...

"I don't expect you'll be showing up at my doorstep again," Mustafa said raising his brows, the hint of a threat in his dark eyes.

"Trust me; I'm not here for Angie."

Mustafa smirked. "I suppose that thing you're with, she's your new woman?"

"She's not my woman. She's my business partner." I twirled the goblet on the tablecloth—Egyptian silk and handwoven lace—Angie always had expensive taste.

"She's pretty, in a dangerous kind of way. You always did like a little danger with your women, didn't you?"

My eyes returned to Mustafa. He sat back, his arms crossed over his belly, smiling at me. As if Angie had told him secrets. As if he knew more about me than I thought he did.

He was wrong.

Nobody knew me. Nobody had secrets on me. I was in debt to nobody.

"Well, she's made you a beautiful home, anyway." I checked my watch.

Deacon should be here in the next twenty minutes. I'd texted him from the road. Mustafa would make his move soon. The sooner the better.

I scanned the room—there was a closet. He'd probably fit in it.

"You'll give me a tour, won't you?" I pushed back my chair. "I'd love to see the kitchen. You know how I enjoy cooking," I said, standing.

Mustafa stayed seated, his eyes narrowed.

"You think I'd poison your food?" His voice came out gruff, angry, his cheeks flushed.

"Don't sound so insulted, Mustafa."

"You think I'd have Angie watch you die right at her table?" He gestured toward the plate that Angie had abandoned. "You show up here, unannounced, and refuse to eat my food because you think it's poisoned?" His voice rose. I kept my knees bent and fingers loose—ready for whatever happened. "You expect me to accept this?" Sweat beaded on his forehead, and his nostrils flared like a bull about to charge.

A small smile pulled at my lips, but I held them in line. His jealousy offered me an advantage. "What are you going to do about it?"

He stood, a pistol appearing in his hand. *Too loud.* He couldn't use it. Not if he didn't want Angie seeing my body, as he claimed. I believed that. He did love her.

I pulled my knife, and he grinned. "Bringing a knife to gun fight— isn't that some kind of American saying?" I let a smile slip across my lips but didn't answer. I couldn't use the knife, as much as he couldn't use his gun. The only way to kill Mustafa was to strangle him. If I spilled blood all over the dining room, Angie, or another member of his house- hold, would notice immediately and Sydney and I needed time to get away.

Mustafa gestured with his weapon—a matte black piece with a snub nose. It looked like something of his own design. "Walk," he said, indicating I should move toward the kitchen, in the opposite direction that Angie and Sydney had taken.

I slowly moved around the table, his pistol following me. At the end, closest to the kitchen doors, I paused. Waiting for him to come closer. "Keep walking," he said, gesturing with his chin.

The table was still between us. I needed to make him come at me. Give me an opening.

"Angie calls me sometimes, you know?" His color heightened at my taunting words. "And tells me about how she misses me. How she misses what we had."

"Liar."

"You can't satisfy her the way I did." His finger tightened on the trigger. I was balancing on a tight rope—lean too far to one side, and he'd shoot me right here, Angie's feelings be damned. But if I let him lead me deeper into the house—create more distance from Angie—then he'd shoot me there. I had to get him to physically attack me right here. I had to walk the line.

"Do you tie her up the way I did?" I licked my lips, adrenaline seeping into my system. His muscles twitched just before he charged. Mustafa came at me fast for a man of his build. Glasses fell, clinking against silverware as he brushed the table. His shoulder rammed into my chest, driving me across the room. We fell against the wall with a thud that shook the chandelier, making it jangle.

He stepped back and threw a hook, his fist powering into my side. The breath whooshed out of me, and I dropped my knife, twisting my body and bringing my hand down in a chopping motion onto his wrist. The gun clattered to the floor.

Then it was just two bodies—two men—fighting for their lives. We grappled, entwined in each other, almost like lovers.

His jealousy fueled him, and he kept me against the wall. I blocked him, keeping my arms close to my side, fists up by my face as he pummeled me, landing punishing blows against my forearms and biceps. The great Muhammad Ali used to call this defensive style of fighting his Rope a Dope—let his opponent punch himself out, then move in for the kill.

Mustafa's breath grew ragged, and his meaty fists slowed, their power waning. I bent my knees and came up with a powerful uppercut that sent him spiraling backward, his chin up, neck exposed.

I kicked him in the stomach, and he fell back onto the table, sending glasses and cutlery spilling onto the floor. *Too loud.* As he brought his arms up to defend himself, I sprang forward, my hands latching onto his throat as tight and deadly as a lion's jaws. My body weight heavy on him, I pressed him into the table.

Mustafa flailed, grabbing at my hands, his eyes wide. My height gave me the advantage—he couldn't reach past my shoulders. I stared into his gaze, the panic there fortifying my strength. *I had him.*

Desperately he grabbed at the table, found a fork and brought it up, driving it into my shoulder. Adrenaline hid the pain from me. His face went purple as his lips turned blue.

His hands searched the table again, desperate now as his eyes lost focus. They found nothing and returned to my fingers, weakly pulling at them.

His eyes fluttered closed as his hands went limp. He was out, but I could still feel his pulse beneath my hands—fluttering and vulnerable. If I held his throat a little longer, I'd kill him. A thrill of pure power radiated through me, flushing my skin and shortening my breaths.

Should I spare him for Angie? Let her keep this man she appeared to adore, who loved her back? Or kill him, to protect myself from future attacks? *Me or her?*

Stepping back, I pulled the fork from my shoulder and rubbed at the spot. My thick canvas shirt had protected me, and the wound was minor.

I gagged Mustafa with a napkin and bound his wrists and feet before dragging his limp body to the closet and folding him into it. Sweating and out of breath, I checked my watch. Deacon would arrive any minute.

Footsteps in the hall: high heels, heavy boots, and the click of a dog's nails. My eyes scanned the dining room—the table askew, cutlery and broken glass on the floor.

The door burst open and Angie fell through, fear written across her face, Sydney following close behind, her gun drawn. She aimed it at me.

"Don't move, asshole."

I looked into her eyes. They were hazy.

She was no longer under her own control.

CHAPTER SEVEN
WALK THE ROAD

Mulberry

A storm blustered and wailed through the dark of night into the early morning, leaving the grass soaked and silvery wet. The sun shone now though, catching each droplet and making it shine.

The sea of uniforms at my father's funeral undulated with movement. *A sea of brothers.* I ranked among them, my graduation from the academy only two weeks behind me.

I'd lost him so quickly.

But at least he was there to see me take my oath and join the New York City Police Department.

My mother's thin arm through mine felt fragile. She'd aged rapidly in the last year, as a bout of pneumonia had turned into a lung infection and all the years of smoking left her wheezing and weak.

She was going to die, too.

My chest constricted with grief, and I forced it out, straightening my shoulders and standing tall and strong next to her—a pillar of support on the outside and a waterfall of grief on the inside.

The casket glistened in the morning sun. My father's second wife, Grace, sat in a folding chair across from it. *His widow.*

Grace held my sister in her arms. The infant slept in a bundle of black blankets, her little hand pale against her mother's dress. Tears streaked down Grace's face, her eyes swollen with grief.

My chest tightened, thinking of how that baby would never know her father. Would never know the brave man who fought to keep her city and fellow citizens safe.

The officers folded the flag, backs straight, faces solemn, and placed it in his widow's lap. I couldn't keep my eyes off her. Her auburn hair fell in waves around her shoulders, the navy dress stiff and ill-fitted, loose and bunching at her hips—like she'd just bought it, or she'd changed so much since the purchase that it no longer looked like her own clothing.

My father's widow, only ten years older than me, was beautiful, and I could see why he wanted her. Could see why he was willing to abandon my mother to have her.

She took the flag, awkwardly, holding it against her breasts along with my sister.

The little girl woke up and began to cry softly, scratching at Grace's dress, reaching for her breasts.

My mother squeezed my arm, and I looked down at her. She was watching, too, her face set in bitter lines of regret and jealousy.

That was her flag.

She'd been married to my father for twenty years, and his widow had been married to him for four. *Four.*

And yet Grace held the flag. She would get his pension. She was his widow, and my mother his ex-wife.

The crowd began to disperse, men coming over to me and shaking my hand, patting me on the shoulder and telling me what a good man my father had been.

My mother excused herself to head back to the car. I watched her cross the cemetery, alone, her thin shoulders stooped, her black dress hanging off her quickly deteriorating body.

I needed to speak to Grace, despite my mother's wish that I ignore her—that I pretend like my sister wasn't my blood.

The mourners and well-wishers parted when I approached.

Grace's gaze found mine, emerald green eyes surrounded by thick lashes and red-rimmed with grief. Under the mourning suppressed rage simmered, and when her eyes met mine, it seemed to ignite.

Her mouth turned into a deep frown, and her fingers tightened on the bundle in her arms, as if I would try to grab the little girl from her. Or perhaps it was the flag she feared I'd try to take.

"I'm sorry for your loss," I said, my voice a deep baritone, the richness of it so different than when I first met her—my voice had cracked and squeaked at her wedding. I had been a boy. I stood before her now, a man. The man my father had raised.

Perhaps we could find some sort of solace together. She'd reached out to me in my youth, and to honor my mother, I had treated her like an enemy combatant. *But death changed everything.*

This was the first time I'd seen my sister, and my gaze searched the blankets for a closer look at her.

"You've joined the police force," she said, her chin rising to indicate my uniform, crisp and clean, brand new.

My chest swelled with pride and I nodded. "Yes."

"Don't get shot like your father did." Her words stole my breath—the pain sharp and unexpected.

The men standing around us turned, uncomfortable with the rawness of her emotion, the ferocity of her attack.

"No one plans to die in the line of duty," I said slowly, searching for words, holding back my anger and hurt and trying to extend her sympathy. "But that's the risk we take when we stand up for those weaker than us."

Her eyes brimmed with tears. "What about Charlene? What about my little girl? Doesn't she matter? Don't I matter?"

"Of course you do." My fingers curled into my palm so that I wouldn't reach out and touch her. So that I wouldn't try and comfort her.

She trembled in the March winds and held my gaze. "If your father had really loved me, if he'd really cared about his daughter, he wouldn't have put himself in danger. He would've made sure that he was here for us."

I pulled in a slow breath, witnessing for the first time the chasm between our understandings of my father. She stood on one side of a canyon, and I on the other—the space between us an abyss. There was no bridge strong enough to span the distance.

"My father was a good man. He loved you enough to leave me." The edge in my voice was unintentional. *My father would not want me speaking to his widow this way.* I dropped my eyes down to my shoes. I'd polished them to a bright sheen, and now dew beaded on the black leather.

"He loved you very much. And he loved his daughter. And he loved me. But he did what he believed was right and necessary." I raised my eyes to her again.

She held my gaze, anger and the cold breeze shaking her. "You're a fool, just like him. You want to be honorable. But all you're going to be is dead."

She turned quickly, almost stumbling. I reached out a hand to steady her, but she whipped away from me, and threw over her shoulder one last barb. "I don't ever want to see you again. I don't ever want to hear from you. You leave my daughter alone."

I watched her storm across the cemetery, her gait steady, rage propelling her forward.

So different than my own mother. Young and angry, versus dying and defeated.

I stood there, watching her go until she was just a tiny figure climbing into a black car.

Then I turned around and looked at the casket in the ground and grief welled up inside me so that I could hardly breathe.

I heard my father's voice.

Son, you know what the right thing to do is. There is a price to honor. A price we all must pay. But it's worth it.

Would he still agree? My father laid in a coma from the time he was shot until the time he died. He'd been so still, so silent but for the beeping of the machines ticking off the beats of his heart...until it failed and the machines fell quiet.

I'd never hear his voice again.

It was up to me to forge my path, to make my own decisions.

I turned away from the casket, from his memory, and strode off toward the wake, toward the sea of blue that waited for me—my brothers in arms. They'd support me now and always.

I had faith in them.

EK

Anita

The hard-packed earth of the running trail cushioned each footfall. My breath came in harsh pants as I sprinted through the jungle. Music of the animals around me, birds squawking and rodents scuttling, broke through the thoughts circling in my mind.

Should we release the tape?

Will Zerzan do it anyway?

How should we respond to the wave of unexpected publicity?

Joyful Justice's PR and marketing was my responsibility, my obsession, my passion. The public's opinion of us wavered between terrorists and saviors.

While we never tried to recruit new members as Isis and other organizations did, we *did* try to convince the world that what we were doing was the right thing.

People found us through the website joyfuljustice.com. It was started months after Sydney Rye aka Joy Humbolt murdered the Mayor of New York to avenge her brother's death. Joy Humbolt, dog walker, single young woman, broke into the mayor's home and killed him, because the authorities wouldn't touch him. Then she fled the country. Two years later Joy Humbolt was believed to have died in Mexico, the circumstances suspicious and the body burned beyond recognition.

Joyfuljustice.com started as a place where people bore witness to injustice and gave each other solace, but had slowly become a place where people planned action against wrongdoers. Once Dan, with his brilliance and unparalleled computer abilities, got involved, it morphed into something organized, dangerous, and very illegal.

The running path opened up, curving around the edge of the inactive volcano, the trees fading as the path grew narrow. To my left, black rock descended to the ocean at a steep grade. Waves smashed against the island's edge. To my right the volcano rose up, its slopes green and lush. Even at this close distance it was impossible to perceive what took place inside.

I slowed to a walk and drank from my water bottle. Whenever I had a tough decision to make, or was stuck on a problem, I'd go for a run.

I also knew that Dan and his morning paddleboarders would be at the beach I was headed toward. I'd never met anyone like Dan. Not only did he run Joyful Justice's strategic operations, use his incredible hacking abilities to gain vital insights, but he also found time to care…

He was in love with Sydney Rye.

When I met them, they'd been living together in a hut in Goa, India. Sydney saved my life. *I owed her so much.*

A group of sex traffickers I was investigating captured me. They were toying with me, about to rape me before murdering me, when Sydney dashed out of the darkness and saved my life.

I told her what had happened, the full extent of my investigation, and she joined me to take down the leader and his organization. When I was captured again, and suffered for days at the hands of his men, Sydney never gave up trying to find me. And Dan helped her.

He followed her lead.

How many men as brilliant and strong as Dan Burke were willing to follow the lead of a woman?

My ex-husband flashed across my mind. Tom. Tall, handsome, from a well-known and respected English family, Tom ruled the world with the easy grace of one born to do so. Would he follow a woman? Me?

I shook my head, trying to clear him from my thoughts. I'd left him because I couldn't live in his shadow. Needed to stand on my own two feet. Not that he'd even tried to overshadow me, but he couldn't help it. The world made him bigger and more important than me.

I worked my way down the path toward the beach and crouched in the shade of a tree, watching the small figures on their paddleboards moving to the shore.

Laughter reached me across the water, and I saw one of Dan's engineers, Gregory, throw his head back.

It was a smaller crew today, only six of them.

Dan had everyone working overtime trying to identify the Her Prophet, in addition to their regular duties.

It wasn't unusual for him to ask so much of his crew; however, for him to let them out of their outdoor activities was rare.

The waves brought them in, and using his paddle and bending his knees, Dan surfed along a wave's edge, directing himself to the shore and then dropping into waist-high water.

He flicked his head, shaking his long hair off his face. It caught the sunlight, reflecting it back. His arms around his board, Dan waded in, the tendons in his forearms popping with the effort.

I waited in the shade of a tree, needing to speak with him but enjoying watching him too much to say anything. There was something safe about watching Dan...lusting after him.

The Supreme Lord said: It is lust alone, which is born of contact with the mode of passion, and later transformed into anger. Know this as the sinful, all-devouring enemy in the world.

I didn't have to worry about Dan—we could never be together, even if we wanted to. I could just look.

Droplets of water fell from Dan's hair, sliding over his corded shoulders and running down his sculpted chest. He emerged from the water and dropped his board onto the sand, laying his paddle next to it and then reached up to the sky in a stretch.

Spotting me, Dan smiled. "Hey," he said.

I stood and brushed the sand off my jogging shorts. "I was out for a run and figured I'd meet you." I shrugged. "I was wondering if you'd made any progress on finding *Her*."

His grin grew wider.

"I'm pretty sure I found her."

My heartbeat picked up its pace. "Seriously?"

Dan nodded. "Give me a second to put my board away."

I nodded. He carried it over to the paddleboard holder set against the rocks, his back muscles defined and glistening in the bright morning light. He slid his board in, and then, saying goodbye to the rest of his crew, jogged back to me.

He slipped on a pair of flip-flops and grabbed a water bottle but remained shirtless.

My eyes ran over the contours of his chest, lingering on the hard ridges of his abdominal muscles as we fell into step next to each other on the path back to the command center.

"So," Dan said, his voice high with excitement. He sounded almost like a teenage boy with a good bit of gossip.

I was happy to see the broad smile on his face. He'd seemed morose lately. Overworked. No doubt worried about Sydney.

"So what we did is crosscheck all of the flight information we could find going into Syria, Iraq, Iran, and Turkey in the last four years, with the list of surgeons in every country that has it available."

When Dan said "available" he meant that their servers were hooked up to the Internet, not that the information was readily available to the public.

"Now here's the thing—we know from the information Robert Maxim sent us that whoever worked on Sydney in the field was a hell of a surgeon."

"Sydney is also in really good shape," I noted.

Dan nodded and continued. "The point is that we're not looking at a huge pool of people here. Especially since we're also only looking at women." I flinched—not that I didn't know that there were a lot more male surgeons than female. But just that it was so fucking wrong.

"So, I found—well, I should say, Gregory found...technically, Gregory's script found."

I let Dan go on, explaining to me in overwhelming detail the brilliance of Gregory's script, which had done the narrowing down for them. I understood bits and pieces of it, but really I just let the up and down of his rich voice lull me. What I needed was a name—a person—in order to humanize this prophet. I didn't care how Dan got it for me.

"I'm pretty sure her name is Rida Dweck. She's Syrian-born, is off-the-charts brilliant, went back to Syria right before shit hit the fan and hasn't been heard from since."

I stopped walking. Dan had gone another three steps, his head down, as he continued to talk. But his gaze traveled up and back to me. When his eyes landed on my face, he cocked his head and his brow furrowed in concern.

"You okay?"

"I know a Rida Dweck."

"You do?"

"She was at Imperial College London while I was at University of Westminster."

"1994 to '98," Dan said, rattling off the years that Rida Dweck attended ICL.

"We were friends." My voice came out a soft whisper as her face danced out from my memories.

Dan walked back to me, the smell of salt and ocean coming with him. A smattering of sand caught in his chest hair glittered in the sunlight that diamonded through the jungle foliage.

"That's wild," he said. "I knew you and she were in London at the same time, but it never occurred to me..."

"We met at a yoga class. She was a very serious student." I looked up at him. "She wasn't religious at all. I mean, her family was Muslim but..."

"No, according to everything I've found, she didn't wear a headscarf and had basically given up her religion."

"It caused a rift with her family," I said, remembering our long talks. Rida was older than me, but we shared brown skin in a very white world. Neither of our families approved of us. And both of us wanted big things, wanted to help people.

We'd slowly lost touch. But if someone had asked me, *Do you know Rida Dweck, is she a friend of yours?* I would have said yes. "I can't believe it's her."

"Why not?" Dan asked.

"The Her Prophet is a zealot. A diehard feminist. Rida was none of those things. She just wanted to help people. She didn't like conflict. Was brilliant and quiet and bookish."

"People change," Dan said, his voice edged with hard-learned lessons.

My neck felt hot and my brain buzzed. "I know people change," I said.

"Maybe she had an experience..." Dan continued to hold my gaze.

I had an experience that changed me.

"She can't be the only person on your list," I said.

Dan shook his head. "No, there are a few others, but she's the best candidate. She was assumed dead, you know?"

"I didn't." The ground under my feet felt shaky. In my mind, Rida had stayed the same brilliant, quiet surgeon she'd always been. *I'd put Rida in a safe bubble, and Dan was breaking the glass.*

HER PROPHET

Because you didn't
follow the rules
something bad happened.
Everything bad is
always happening. Everything
has already happened
and is yet to come.
You are everything.
...pure and good.
True or false?

CHAPTER EIGHT
STORIES TOLD, MEMORIES FOLD

April

They fed me, offered me use of the shower and loaned me clean clothing
—a pair of sweatpants and T-shirt. Then we all sat down in the rectory.

"Thank you," I said. "Thank you for your help, and for listening to
me." Taking in a deep breath, I closed my eyes for a moment and gathered my thoughts. *Where to begin?*

"My daughter went missing in Isis territory." The women gasped.
They were good Christians—Cynthia, Madeline, Debbie, and Nancy
traveled from Fort Lauderdale, Florida, to this gathering place for Syrian
refugees just over the Turkish border to bring the message of Jesus
Christ to the people here. They knew about the ills of Isis, but not about
the prophet...it was my job to tell them.

"We were estranged, Joy and I." My lips pursed as memories of our
life together flashed through my mind—her rebellious teenage years
while I searched for sobriety, the split in our relationship when she
moved out, after refusing to acknowledge Jesus as her Lord and Savior.
Joy forced me to turn away from her...or so I'd thought. "I lost my son,"
My throat closed with pain, but I opened my eyes and pushed on. *This
was more important than me.* "He was murdered several years ago."

"I'm so sorry," Cynthia said, leaning forward and placing a warm hand on my knee, her blue eyes welling with tears.

I nodded and went on. "When I heard my daughter was missing, something inside me changed." I cleared my throat. "I didn't know if it was the devil or the Lord, I just knew I had to go look for her."

Nancy nodded, popping a mint into her mouth. She had mousy, brown hair cut into a neat bob. Her lips were painted coral, the same tone as the blouse she wore. "How did you get across the border?" she asked, her chocolate brown eyes round with admiration and curiosity.

"I couldn't have done it without the Lord," I said. "Until very recently, I lived with the devil always whispering to me."

The women all nodded, their mouths turned down in knowing frowns. *They must hear the devil's voice, too.*

"He told me to drink."

Color stole over Debbie's neck and cheeks.

"I drank to excess, even as I was desperate to find my daughter. I drank to where I didn't remember what I did."

Madeline clucked her tongue, the sound at once admonishing and sympathetic. The oldest in the group, Madeline's silver hair was pulled back into a tight bun, and large square spectacles made her look almost like she was behind a window—hidden from the world, but watching it.

"When I woke up," I continued, "the Lord had brought me to a man who was willing to take me across the border."

I left out the part about how I slept with him in exchange for that passage, images of his face above mine and his weight against me bringing heat to my chest.

"I did not find my daughter for some time, but I met a group of young women. Barely women at all, teenagers really, who had escaped Isis."

Cynthia nodded, leaning closer, listening intently.

"They were Yazidi," I looked around to see if they knew what that meant. Solemn nods told me they did know about this small religious group whose beliefs combine Islam, Christianity and other traditions. "Isis believes Yazidis worship the devil, and therefore they had the right to kill the men, and enslave the women. It was former slaves who told me about the prophet. A woman."

The room became very still.

"The prophet is Her. We are all Her."

Cynthia frowned. "I don't understand."

I gestured toward the tote bag I'd seen her slip her iPad into. "Let me show you a video."

Cynthia handed over the device, and I navigated to YouTube, finding the video easily.

The screen filled with the image of a cloaked woman, everything covered, including her eyes. I turned the iPad so that we could all see it, and hit play. The covered figure spoke in Arabic, her voice distorted, and English subtitles appeared at the bottom of the screen.

"I am Her," the woman said. "I am all of you. You are all me. We all follow the one true God, who has come to us, now, in this time of caliphate, to lead us to the Promised Land. Men and women are equal. But they will not know it—the world will not acknowledge it—until we do. We decide our own value." The prophet touched a gloved finger to her temple. "I wear this burka to remind you that we are nameless, face-less, female. We are all one. I am Her. You are Her. We are all Her. I am your prophet, and this is our new beginning. We decide our value." The woman on the screen paused, and a tense silence filled the rectory. "Spread the message, change the world, release the wolf."

The video ended, and I laid the iPad in my lap.

"What does she mean, 'release the wolf'?" Cynthia asked.

I navigated on the iPad until I found the image I wanted. It was a symbol that I'd helped paint all over Isis-controlled territory: a wolf's profile, its lip raised in a snarl, with a woman's silhouette set inside it—the symbol of the prophet. I turned the iPad around for them to see. "We must fight for our value," I said. "Be willing to release the power inside ourselves in order to make it clear that we are equals, not chattel, not slaves…that we are wolves, capable of great things. An endless flock of wolves."

Cynthia nodded slowly, Madeline pursed her lips, and Debbie swal-lowed audibly—fear written across her face.

"Is the prophet Muslim?" Nancy asked.

I shook my head. "She is a prophet. Muslims, Christians, Yazidis… many religions believe in prophets."

"What is this prophet's name?"

"She is nameless, faceless. *Her.*"

"But," Cynthia said, "what makes her a prophet? Just because she says so?"

"No, she has produced a miracle. Brought a woman back from the dead. There are witnesses…I, myself, have seen this Miracle Woman." I paused; the women leaned toward me. *I had them.* "My daughter is the Miracle Woman. And I fought by her side in the battle of Surama."

They stared at me, eyes wide, mouths slack—I'd shocked them.

"Your daughter?" Cynthia asked.

"Yes," I nodded, feeling the weight of this great gift from God on my shoulders. "I have been tasked with spreading the message."

"But—" Cynthia cast her blue eyes down into her lap, where her fingers entwined, her knuckles whitening as she pressed them together. "This prophet says that we decide our own value." She raised her gaze to mine. "I believe that God decides our value."

"Yes," I said, my voice rising with the passion I felt. "He has created us, and as his creations our value is clear."

"But, then what do we decide?"

"We decide whether we acknowledge it, whether we see what God has done, and admit that we have as much value as anyone else. Whether we have faith. Or we ignore God, and we continue to live in the shadow of men."

Debbie giggled nervously—a strange sound on a woman close to my age.

"What makes you think you're not as valuable as a man?" I asked, turning to her, my voice harsh with accusation.

"Oh no, I know I am. I know I have value." Her eyes darted to her friends, and she blushed deeply.

"Women give birth. We create life."

"Well, we need men for that," Madeline said with a laugh—trying to lighten the mood.

80

My hands tighten into fists. "Of course." I forced a deep breath, searching for calm. *All is as it is meant to be.* "We have as much value as men. We are equal. Not more or less. But only we can decide that."

"But, if we are equal to men, then why did He make us weaker?" Nancy asked. She fiddled with her package of mints so that they jangled against the metal.

"Did he make us weaker?" I responded, turning to her, holding her gaze.

Nancy's green eyes darted around the room, looking for the answer in her fellow travelers' expressions. "I mean," she cleared her throat. "My husband can pick up much heavier things than me."

"Yes, and my husband is much better with figures than I am. I don't even try with that kind of thing." Madeline waved her hand at the idea that she would try and deal with *numbers.*

"And how many meals has he cooked?" I asked Madeline. She stared through her glasses at me as her manicured fingers rose to her neck, where a string of pearls circled her like a collar.

"Oh, he doesn't cook?" I went on.

"And laundry, does he do laundry?"

Madeline shook her head. "But that stuff's easy."

I laughed. "Is it? Is it so easy?"

"Well, not as hard as making money." Madeline sat up straighter, defending her husband's superiority. *It is easier to defend others than ourselves.*

"Are you saying that you think your husband has more value than you?" I asked her, determined to make Madeline give me a straight answer.

Her lips pursed. "He makes more money than me."

"And is that how value is decided, do you think?"

"Well, the Lord blesses those in his favor with many different things, including money." She nodded to herself, repeating words I'd heard Bill say thousands of times. *To give to the church is like a savings account with God. He will repay you tenfold.*

"So, you think the fact that you haven't made money means the Lord hasn't blessed you?"

"Oh no, I'm very blessed. I have two wonderful, grown children, a wonderful husband. I'm very blessed." Madeline smiled, her family a cocoon of satisfaction that gave her the strength to meet my gaze.

"So then you must have as much value as your husband, in the eyes of the Lord." She blinked, her mouth parting, but nothing came out. "What does it feel like in here?" I touched my hand to my chest, laying it over my heart. I felt that steady thump, a drum beat—a reminder of the strength and wisdom of the women I had walked with in Isis territory.

These women in front of me now, so like my former self, lived in a world where they were *almost* equal.

Where they *almost* had the same value as men.

And the gap was so small that these women readily accepted it.

They hadn't even realized that they were treated like less—that they treated *themselves* like less. *Took pride in their husbands instead of themselves.*

In Isis-controlled territory, the oppression of women was as obvious as a marching band...in the West it was as subtle and constant as a heartbeat.

I'd just come from where it was obvious, and I needed to go back to where it wasn't.

And then the Lord sent me a vision. I was on the stage, the stage that Bill stood on, but I was the one behind the pulpit. It was my name in bright lights behind me. *I was the preacher.*

Yes!

My vision was so clouded with this premonition that I didn't hear Madeline's response.

"Sorry, what did you say?" I asked, bringing the woman back into focus.

Her hand was over her chest; she was nodding slowly. "I think I do have as much value. As much value as a man."

"Then you do," I said.

"I think I do, too," Cynthia said, her voice strong. "I lost my husband. My children are grown. But I live on...and I've wondered why."

"To help me spread this message," I said.

Her eyes lit with new faith. "I believe you," she said.

"Me, too," Debbie said, her cheeks pink.

I turned to Nancy, whose face had gone pale. "What about you?" I asked.

She nodded slowly. "Me, too."

EK

Mulberry

She pushed back the hair from my brow and laughed.

"What?" I asked, capturing her wrist and kissing it.

"You're starting to get some gray," she said and grinned, lying back against the pillow. Soft morning light filtered in through the windows. Traffic passed on the street below, a low murmur as familiar to me as my heartbeat. *I loved this city.*

My brow furrowed. "That's funny to you? Your husband getting old amuses you?"

She smiled, her dimple appearing, and my heart ached with how much I loved her.

Sandy pulled her lip between her teeth, and her green gaze turned serious. She shrugged and looked down at my hand still holding hers. "What would you think about, maybe..." she looked up at me, "leaving the force soon?"

I frowned and dropped her hand, running it through my hair. "You know I love what I do."

She sat up, the sheets falling away from her body, exposing her soft skin, the elegant curve of her waist. "But, you could go into the private sector, where people also need protection. You'd make so much more money."

"What?" My voice came out harsher than I meant it, and she flinched. "Work for a guy like Robert Maxim, for Fortress Global Investigations—be a hired gun?" *Never.*

Her face hardened. "I want to have a family. And I want you to be around to raise our kids."

"Nothing's going to happen to me."

"You don't know that." Her voice rose. "Look what happened—" She stopped herself before saying my father's name. But the shadow of his death filled the room.

My alarm sounded, an annoying beep-beep, and I threw off the covers, rolling away from her. "I have to get to work. We can finish this conversation later."

EK

It took Herculean effort to lift my eyelids. How did they get sealed shut? Why did my head feel so fuzzy, and my body throb with disuse and meddling pains?

I got my eyes open, but the lids slid right down again before I could focus. Sucking in a deep breath, I steeled myself for another attempt. As I lay there in the darkness behind my lids, gathering my strength, I heard the beeping of my alarm clock.

I needed to get my damn eyes open.

A deep breath in, and I again lifted the lids. Straining to keep them open, my pupils dilated, bringing the world into focus...a white ceiling.

My lids tried to close again. *I couldn't let them.*

Not before I turned my head. I slowly shifted my gaze. A machine next to me showed a mountain range of heartbeats dancing out on the screen.

What?

My eyes closed, but I forced them open again quickly. Practically a blink this time.

Wriggling my fingers against rough sheets, I turned my head in the other direction. A man slept in a chair next to me, his breathing even and deep.

Tall and broad, the stranger's dark skin looked almost purple in the stark light of the hospital room.

I was in a hospital bed.

How did I get here?

I cleared my throat, planning to ask the question out loud.

The man woke, honey brown eyes blinking into awareness. When he saw me staring at him, a wide smile transformed his face.

"You're awake." His voice was accented, lyrical and smooth. He sounded West African— maybe Senegalese—that mix of French and English I'd heard on the streets of Le Petit Sénégal in Harlem.

"Yeah, I'm awake," I said, my voice coming out rough, like I hadn't used it in some time.

"I'll get the doctor," the man said, rising to stand. He was over six feet tall, broad, wearing jeans and a T-shirt that fit him like he was a model. Who was this guy? He seemed to think I knew him. Maybe he was a nurse. But the gold bracelets on his wrist and the fine material of his silk T-shirt, matched with the casual denim, suggested he was a guest visiting me, a friend.

I'd never seen Model Man before in my life.

He moved to the door and opened it, then turned back and threw me another brilliant smile, like he was at the end of a runway, doing one final look back for the audience. "The nurse is right down the hall."

He stepped out, and the door swished closed behind him, as if they were on the same spring, my eyes slid closed with the door.

I took several deep breaths in the darkness, my brain turning over on itself. *Nothing made sense.* Wasn't I just getting out of bed with Sandy? I must have had an accident…

The door swished open again, interrupting my train of thought. Prying open my eyes, I found Model Man returning with a petite nurse. She had caramel-colored skin and wore a green head scarf that brought out the flecks of color in her brown eyes.

"Mr. Mulberry. You're awake."

"Yeah."

"The doctor will be here in just a moment." Model Man hovered behind her as she looked at my machines. I followed her gaze. The mountain range seemed to be holding steady. She touched a bag, and I noticed the lettering wasn't English. Was that Turkish?

Was I in Turkey?

"What's going on?" I asked.

The woman smiled down at me, a closed-lip smile, friendly but restrained. The answer wasn't a happy one. "The doctor will be here in a moment; he'll explain everything."

The door swung open, and a tall, thin, balding man walked in. Thick glasses drooped down his nose, and he pushed them up as he approached, smiling at me.

"Mr. Mulberry, I'm Dr. Dale Mitchell. I'm a neurologist, and I've been a part of your team since you arrived here in Istanbul."

"Istanbul? How did I get to Istanbul?"

"What's the last thing you remember?" the doctor asked as he pulled out a penlight, shining it into my eyes. I shied away from the bright light and held out a hand. My arm felt weightless, strange. I must be on some sort of drugs.

"Mr. Mulberry, I'll need to look at your pupils. You've sustained some injuries, and I want to check on your brain function." The guy smiled.

Check on my brain? Was this guy trying to get punched in the face?

"He's a friend of Robert's," Model Man said, nodding, as though that meant I should trust him. Like I should trust any of these people.

"Robert who?" I croaked.

"Robert Maxim," the doctor said, turning his penlight to my pupils again.

"Robert Maxim?" The owner of Fortress Global? We barely knew each other, and what we did know of each other, we didn't like.

I batted the flashlight away. "What the hell is going on here? Where's my wife?" Dr. Dale cocked his head, and Model Man frowned.

Oh, my God, were we in a car accident? Is Sandy gone?

"From what I understand," Dale said, chewing on his lip for a moment. "Hmm."

"What the hell is going on here?" I said, pushing myself up to sit higher. The nurse hurried over with a pillow and shoved it behind my back. Then she pointed out that I could adjust the bed using a controller in the side bar. She offered me a small smile. She was used to dealing with men like me—frustrated men in hospital beds.

"You were in a battle. You've been injured. It seems that you might have lost some time," Dale said.

"Lost time? A battle?" I looked down at myself. My broad chest looked okay, tapered to a waist, that was good news. My dick appeared to still be there. Excellent. My eyes traveled lower.

My left leg stopped above my knee.

It was some sort of horrible trick. I bent over, feeling tightness in my back and when my fingers touched the nub, pain shot through me.

"I lost my leg." The words came out flat.

"But hey, we thought you might have lost your brain, too, so you're doing pretty good," Dr. Dale said with a smile.

Seriously, was he trying to get punched in the face? My eyes flickered over to Model Man. He was looking at Dale like he wanted to punch him, too.

It was definitely possible that me and this guy were friends, even if he did look like something straight out of GQ.

But where was Sandy? Where was my wife?

What the hell was going on?

CHAPTER NINE
BATTLES WAGED, TEMPLES STAGED

Sydney

Lightning sizzled in the corners of my vision, and thunder sounded so loudly that I could barely hear. Sweat slicked my palm, making my grip on the pistol tighten. Why was I aiming a gun at Robert?

What the hell was happening?

Fuck!

My finger trembled; it wanted to pull the trigger. *Part of me wanted him dead.*

Blue's low growl joined the thunder and helped to settle me. Robert stared at me over the top of my gun.

He knew I didn't have control.

A shiver ran over my skin as a cold wind blew up my spine.

"Robert." My voice came out forced, rough with tension. *She's strangling me.*

"Sydney." Robert took a step forward, his palms open and low, showing me he wasn't holding a weapon. But he had a pistol and knife on each hip. He could reach them quickly.

The thwap of an approaching helicopter broke through the rumble of thunder, and Robert's eyes darted to the window behind me, which looked out onto the lawn.

"Deacon is here. We'll just be on our way." He had control of himself. His voice was smooth, slick, dark chocolate. I could practically taste it on my tongue.

"What is wrong with her?" Angie asked, staring at me.

Robert's gaze flicked to his former wife. "What happened?"

Angie huffed, straightening her clingy, red dress, a small tremble in her fingers. *I'd rattled her.* "I was trying to find her something to wear when she pulled that gun on me. She kept saying *I am Her.* What the hell does that mean?" Angie's voice rose high with fear and frustration. "Where is Mustafa?" she asked suddenly, her eyes scanning the room. "What the fuck happened here?" Her accent suddenly sound very New York.

The dining room lay in disarray; glasses broken on the floor, cutlery askew. The salmon had spilled onto one of the chairs, staining the green satin.

Robert took two quick steps and grabbed Angie by the arm. "Tell me what else she said." His head jerked in my direction.

Angie's mouth turned into a deep frown. "You can't talk to me like this, Robert. Not anymore. I'm not your wife."

He shook Angie so hard that her hair danced around her shoulders. "Tell me what she said."

"Ow!" Angie gasped. Her eyes met Robert's gaze, fiery with rage. "She said she wanted to kill you. That you took something from her."

His eyes jumped to me. *I had no idea what she was talking about. I'd lost time again.* I gritted my teeth. *This had to stop.*

"Stop aiming that gun at me," he growled. I lowered my weapon, taking a deep breath, steeling myself.

I was Sydney motherfucking Rye and this losing control shit was over. Over.

Robert's attention returned to Angie. "We're leaving; you'll walk us out. And you're not going to tell anyone what happened until we are long gone."

"Where is Mustafa?" she asked, her eyes darting around the ruined space.

"Alive."

Color drained from Angie's face. "Did you hurt him?" she asked, her voice a low whisper.

Robert shook his head. "He'll be fine." Robert's expression gave nothing away. A quiet ocean under a cloudless sky, capable of awesome destruction but gently lapping at the shore.

"If you hurt him, I'll get you Robert, I swear." Angie's voice firmed, her anger returning. Power radiated off her. *Pure iron will.*

The two held each other's gaze, and Robert smiled slowly. "Oh, sweetheart." His voice was saccharine, maple syrup over banana pancakes. "I always knew you were a vengeful little bitch." He dropped a dollop of whipped cream on top. "It's one of the things I loved about you."

That brought a flush to her cheeks.

Robert Maxim had *loved* this woman.

My heart thudded, as my mind turned to Mulberry lying in that hospital bed, pale, still. *But not dead.* I forced the image away.

I controlled my mind, body, and heart.

Glancing out the window, I saw that the helicopter had landed: a matte black beetle on the golf course-green of the lawn, blades spinning, waiting for us.

Robert wrapped his hand around Angie's bicep and led her toward the door. "Walk your guests out," he said, his voice even.

"You'll pay for this," Angie told him, but she moved with him... followed his commands.

Blue and I fell into step with them, leaving through the big glass doors. The heat hit like a wall, and I began to sweat as we crossed the stone patio onto the grass.

Robert's hand looked relaxed on Angie, like they were friends—as if he was some kind of gentleman and she some kind of lady he was escorting.

Blue's nose touched my hip, drawing my attention. He was looking behind us. Four men, wearing dark suits, looking like gorillas dressed up for a circus act, were following us.

"Robert." My voice sounded calm, controlled.

He looked back and took in the approaching men, his expression retaining its smooth confidence. Our pace remained steady.

"Angie," he said, his voice even, "who are they?"

"Security," she said, her voice worried.

"Why are they following us?"

She swallowed, her elegant throat bobbing. "I'd guess that they don't trust you."

Robert nodded. "It could look like I'm taking Mustafa's wife."

"Seems that way," I said. My pistol still in my hand probably wasn't helping matters.

"Stop!" One of them yelled. He raised a small machine gun from under his arm.

I did as he asked. Robert and Angie turned as well. Robert pulled Angie in front of him.

Blue's hackles raised as the four men caught up to us. "Everything okay?" Angie asked, her voice different—talking to the staff.

"Ma'am. Where is Mr. Kilicli?" the lead gorilla asked. His English was accented. Silver at his temples and lines around his eyes made him out as the oldest.

"Back at the house" she replied. "I'm just showing them out."

"Ma'am, Mr. Kilicli did not want them to leave."

"Really?" I asked. "Am I your prisoner?"

My body tensed as I waited a beat for his answer. His dark brown eyes met mine and went slightly rounder as his lips parted. "Not you," he said. "Just him." He used his chin to gesture towards Robert.

The other men moved wider, forming a semi-circle around us. They had not raised their weapons yet. Just Silverback, the muzzle of his weapon aimed low, not at any of us—if he fired it would go straight into the ground at Robert's feet.

The sun heated my back, the lightning sizzling at the edge of my vision stayed at bay, the adrenaline in my system chasing it away, lending me the strength I'd need.

"In that case, I'm gonna go," I said with a shrug.

Robert didn't look at me. His one hand stayed on Angie's arm, the other loose by his side, right next to his pistol but not even tensed. It would take him a second to get it out. I could take out Silverback before he did. But there were three more. They couldn't risk hitting Angie, though. That's why we were still standing here talking.

"You're free to go," Silverback said, holding my gaze. I turned and headed toward the helicopter, my steps slow, Blue by my side. My hand touched his rough coat and he waited. The helicopter sat about fifty yards away, the blades spinning, and the wind they created just reaching me. We were going to have to incapacitate the entire team. Probably kill them.

A moment of hesitation—did they have children? Wives? Certainly mothers...I was about to break some hearts.

Dropping to my knees, I spun around on them, the grass soft and pliant under me. My aim found Silverback's chest, and I fired. He stumbled back as my bullets hit their mark. I didn't have time to watch him fall, my aim already moving over to the next. His gun rose, but I was faster. The man's head arched back. My arm kept moving.

The last two men were now only one—Robert's pistol was up and smoking. The last bodyguard fired his weapon, the quick rat-tat-tat sending clumps of grass flying right in front of Angie. I'm not sure if Robert or I killed him, but he dropped to his knees, blood pouring from between his eyes before slumping onto the ground with the rest of his team.

Angie screamed. Blue barked. The helicopter thwapped. And thunder rolled.

Adrenaline coursed through me, and I reveled in the feeling for just a moment before rising to my feet. Blue barked once before lunging forward, bounding toward Silverback. The bodyguard struggled to reach for his weapon, just a hand's distance away. Blue landed on him, his canines sinking into the man's wrist, stopping him from grabbing his gun.

Robert took three fast strides, and standing over Silverback, fired into his skull, the shots somehow louder than the others.

Angie's screaming stopped, and she began to collapse. I stepped forward, catching her before she hit the grass. Her face had gone slack, and the stillness transformed her beauty; she looked human and vulnerable lying in my arms, not some fantasy of what a woman should be.

I laid her gently on the grass and glanced up at the fallen men. Blood pooled around them. *Life goes quickly.*

"Let's go," Robert said, his voice as steady as ever.

I turned away from the bodies and moved with him and Blue toward the helicopter.

I recognized the pilot, Deacon, a big Texan with Special Forces training. He sat at the controls, his eyes covered in dark shades. He nodded laconically at me, apparently unfazed by the mayhem that had just happened on the lawn, and I returned the gesture.

Blue, Robert, and I climbed into the helicopter, and it rose up into the sky as the sun beat down on this spot of green paradise in a desolate desert. The bodies left on the lawn—four black forms and one woman in a red dress—looked as strange as the mansion's architecture, as out of place as its trees and gardens.

Robert spoke to Deacon, giving him directions.

"Will Deacon drop us at the cave of the prophet?" I asked.

"Not that close," Robert responded. "It's still Isis territory. We'll need to hike." He held out his hand. "Give me your gun."

"What?" I tightened my grip on it, protective of my weapon, still hot from use.

His cold gaze held mine. "You want to kill me. You can't expect me to make it easy."

"I don't want to kill you. I just saved your fucking life."

"Part of you does."

"You don't trust me?"

"Nobody does." He threw my own words back at me.

I smiled at him, holding his gaze. "Don't worry," I promised. "I've regained control. I'm done with that shit."

The corner of his mouth rose. "You sound certain."

"I am." My voice came out strong, as powerful as the ocean behind Robert's eyes...but my sea boiled hot while his was frozen over. *We made one hell of a team.*

EK

April

My heart hammered as the phone rang. I wrapped the cord around my fingers, turning the flesh between them white.

Sucking in a deep breath, I closed my eyes.

I have value. I decide my value.

"Hello?"

Bill's voice traveled across the distance from where he was in Texas to where I sat, in a hotel in Istanbul. It was that rich baritone, as much as his fiery rhetoric, that had earned him his radio show, which had brought him so much fame and fortune.

"Bill," I said, my voice coming out clear.

"April?"

"Yes, Bill, it's me."

"Where have you been? I've been so worried about you."

Lies. He wasn't worried about me. He was worried about his reputation. About the money I'd taken with me when I left. What it meant that his wife had unceremoniously disappeared.

"Bill, you're going to help me." I stood up and paced away from the bed, my bare feet cool against the wood floor.

"Of course, my love, I'll do anything I can to help you. Where are you? Let me come and get you."

"No, Bill. Our marriage is over. It has been for...what would you say? Five years? Seven? How long after we were married did you start having affairs?"

He stammered for a moment. Unrecognizable words followed finally by "That's ridiculous, April. Are you having a breakdown? Let me come and get you. You know I'm completely loyal."

"You're not loyal. You don't even know what that word means."

"Hey, now." He was getting angry, righteous rage raising his voice. *He was so good at that kind of anger.*

"Don't worry. I have no plans to expose you...as long as you help me."

"Expose what exactly? I'm a man of God. There is nothing to expose."

95

"You think I'm so stupid. You think I didn't build in protections for myself? That I have no evidence of any kind?"

I had no evidence of any kind. But Bill didn't know that.

"Bullshit," he said. But I knew that tone—bluster disguising fear.

"I need my own show. You're going to help me set it up."

"What do you mean, your own show?"

Bill had a radio show, a TV show, and gave live performances regularly. He made millions of dollars each year, which he squandered on fancy hotels, loose women, jewelry, and private jets. I wanted some of those millions, and I wanted to spread the message of *Her*. And I was going to use his devilish ways to do it.

"Let's start with a radio program—we should be able to get that going pretty fast. And then we'll bring in the TV show. Also, I'm ready to start doing live performances immediately."

"April." Now he sounded kind, like he was letting me down easy. "You're not the star of the show, honey. You're...”

"The woman behind the man?"

"Yes, exactly." He seized on it. *I understood.*

"I was. You're absolutely right, Bill. I was. The alcoholic who was saved by the man of God. The single mom who found Jesus and used his strength to push away her gay son. To alienate her liberal daughter."

"Exactly."

"Well, things have changed. I'll be in New York in three days. Meet me at the Omni Hotel. I'll lay it out for you in detail."

I hung up the phone before he could respond.

He had an event at Madison Square Garden in four days. And I was going to give a sermon. American evangelicals were about to get a taste of the prophet *Her*. *I* would spread the message.

I had value.

CHAPTER TEN
CAUSE IS OUR EFFECT

Anita

I stepped out of the shower and grabbed a towel, holding it over my face, letting the hot steam swirl around me.

Rida Dweck.

How could she be the prophet?

Her face came to me, narrow and serious. She wore her long, dark hair pulled back into a braid and always carried a notebook...she liked to write down ideas, to observe people.

How had she gone from such a circumspect observer to a prophet?

In the Hindu tradition we do not believe in prophets as Muslims and Christians do. Enlightenment can be achieved by all of us, not just a chosen few—so in a way we are all prophets.

I shook my head, roughly drying my body. That was ridiculous...

Could Rida really believe she was hearing the voice of God? Had she gone insane?

Why did she return to Syria in the first place? I stepped out into my room and picked up my iPad, navigating to the report Dan had sent me.

Rida returned right before Isis took control of Raqqa. While at the time it was known that Isis existed, the full extent of their power wasn't evident. They hadn't yet swept through western Iraq and northeastern Syria, leaving a trail of destruction, fear, and death in their path.

Rida must have gone home to try to pull her family out when the uprising began against the Assad regime. And failed. Was she imprisoned by Isis? Is that what changed her so radically?

I flipped through the report. It was a collection of loosely related facts: the dates she left London and arrived in Syria. Her school records. Her professional accomplishments. She was as brilliant as I'd always supposed. Rida had been so modest though. So...shy, really.

I'd watched the Her video repeatedly and seen nothing of my friend's mannerisms. The voice was distorted by technology and so I didn't recognize it either.

I dressed quickly in jeans and a T-shirt, then made my way downstairs. We had another council meeting; it was time to decide what to do with the video.

The elevator carried me ten floors underground and opened into the command center. I spotted Dan immediately. He was leaning over a console, pointing to the screen. The man who sat in front of him nodded, the blue light of the computer glow reflecting in his glasses.

Dan looked up, his gaze catching mine, and he gave me a soft smile and a small nod. *He'd meet me in his office.*

I went up the spiral staircase and let myself into his space. It smelled like the salty freshness of the ocean and the plastic of computers. Five monitors filled the large desk that pressed up against the tinted glass wall looking down onto the command center. A laptop sat on the black leather couch. Books and files flowed across the coffee table and onto the floor in a chaotic, organized mess.

A quote from Einstein was taped to one of the monitors...*if a cluttered desk is a sign of a cluttered mind then what is an empty desk a sign of?*

I smiled. Dan's mind was most certainly not empty.

He came in a few minutes later. I'd made myself comfortable on his couch and was flipping through our YouTube channel, checking on the latest comments. They were the classic mix of vile hatred and empowering statements.

The power of the Internet, all contained in the thin tablet I held in my hand, wowed me. In the last decade the power structures of the world had shifted so violently that it felt almost like an earthquake.

When I was a girl, growing up in Gujarat, there was a massive quake. The earth shook for a full three minutes, and when it was done many of the homes around us were rubble. My family's house, over four centuries old, still stood.

The crumbling of structures and loss of life were just the beginning of the mayhem, though. In the wake of the quake, as resources ran out and the authorities were overwhelmed, riots between Hindus and Muslims broke out, tearing our city apart...but it was all eventually put back together.

The Internet was now tearing our world apart. I believed it would all be put back together. *I wanted to be one of the architects.*

"So..." Dan sat in his swivel chair, his long legs out in front of him. He shifted back and forth a few times, as if loosening up his lower back. "Are you ready?"

We still had ten minutes.

"I want to go to London and ask around."

Dan's eyebrows rose. I hadn't left the island in some time. I'd stayed pretty well isolated since the...attack...and its aftermath.

"What do you hope to accomplish?"

I flinched at his question, and Dan cocked his head. "What?"

"Sorry." I shook my head, staring down at my iPad.

You bitches will all rot in hell, God will punish you.

"I'm not sure." I forced myself to meet his gaze. Dan had seen me at my worst. He'd held me when I'd cried, screamed and beat at his chest— a friend, a trusted and loyal man who held me without crossing any lines. I'd needed that so badly. And he'd given it to me. And he never brought it up.

A spark of rage ignited in my stomach, and I tried to put it out, but it quickly kindled into a blaze. "You never talk about what happened," I accused.

Dan's brow furrowed. "Huh?"

"Between us."

Dan slowly sat forward, his elbows coming to his knees, his hands clasped, his gaze holding mine. "Can you elaborate? We've been through a lot together."

I saw Sydney break your heart. And you saw me broken. You saw me lost. And you held me.

"You..."

My face grew hot, and I turned away. Coming to the island was a bad idea. I'd hoped that I'd finally feel safe. That being in this isolated place with Dan would bring me comfort, but my bed was made of broken glass and I had to lie in it.

"I'm listening," Dan said, his voice even, his eyes still on me.

I couldn't hold his gaze. "You saw me at my worst."

"Your bravest, you mean?"

My gaze jumped to his. "What?"

"I've seen you at your bravest." His chair rolled a little toward me. "You're strong, and powerful, and that's how I've always seen you."

Tears burned my eyes, and I shook my head. "I'm a mess, Dan." The words came out choked, the truth burning my throat.

He smiled, small and forgiving. "I like messy."

I hiccupped a laugh and swiped a hand across my eyes, forcing the tears away. "Well, I like organized and orderly." I looked back at him. "And that's why I want to go to London. I need to understand how Rida could change so much."

He nodded. "You think it's totally out of character?"

"Yes. I mean, Dan—" I sat forward and almost grabbed his hands but caught myself. "She was so shy, so studious. She just wanted to be the best surgeon. She wasn't trying to change anyone's mind."

"Wasn't she? In her own way?"

"What do you mean?"

"I mean, a woman from the Middle East being the best surgeon in her graduating class, getting one of the most prestigious positions in her profession...don't you think she changed some minds?"

"But she wasn't *trying* to do that. She was just trying to live her life."

"Like you were?"

"No." I was on the edge of the couch now, my fingers tight around my iPad. "I always wanted to affect people. That's why I was a reporter. I wanted to expose the evil in this world."

"And now you want to destroy that evil."

"Yes!"

He smiled, like I'd just proved his point. I pushed my hair behind my ears and checked my watch. We only had another minute before the call. "If you want to go to London, you should."

I looked up at him from under my lashes; he was turning toward his bank of monitors. "Thanks."

"But just remember," Dan said, as he began to type. "People do change. Often, drastically."

I'd been a brave, brash, reporter dead set on exposing truth. Now, I was a timid, frightened, communications director determined to rid the world of evil. How much had I really changed? How much had those men done to me?

The screens glowed to life and soon Lenox and Merl were up on the monitors. We said our hellos and Lenox updated us on Mulberry's condition. His eyes were rimmed red from exhaustion, but his button-down shirt was freshly pressed.

"He has amnesia," Lenox said, frowning. "His memories stop a decade ago. He still thinks he is married." Dan stiffened next to me. "The doctors have called his ex-wife, and she's agreed to come over."

"So, he doesn't remember any of us?" Merl asked, his voice rough with concern.

"No."

"Have you mentioned Sydney to him?" Dan asked.

Lenox shook his head. "I have not told him about anything, except that we are friends. That we work together. And that it's top secret." Lenox scratched at his jaw. "He may think we work for the government —I have not been at all specific, and an organization like Joyful Justice isn't something he'd consider."

"He's changed a lot in the last decade," Dan said, not looking at me.

"Maybe this is a chance for him to return to who he was before," I said. Everyone looked at me. "I'm just saying, maybe he can, I don't know, return to a normal life." My cheeks heated. *I sounded like an idiot.*

"He won't be ready to return to active duty for some time," Lenox said. "While I don't think we should push him, his memory could come back at any moment."

A silence filled the room. Merl cleared his throat. "Stay with him, Lenox. Let's give this some time to play out. The focus now is his physical recovery."

We all agreed to that and then moved on to discussing the video. "I think we should hold off, not release it," I said. "I've got a response plan in place in case someone else does, but it does nothing for us at this time." The other members of the council agreed with me. *They trusted me totally.*

Then Dan filled them in on what he'd learned about the prophet. "Anita," Dan said, after revealing my connection to her, "wants to head to London and ask around, see what she can find out."

"That concerns me," Merl said. "Won't the CIA and other intelligence agencies be asking around? Won't it be strange for Anita to suddenly show up? I don't want her on their radar."

"I can keep an eye out for that kind of thing," Dan said.

Merl smiled and nodded. "I'm sure, but you can't prevent them from noticing her; all you can do is find out if they have."

"I'm willing to risk it," I said. "This is important to me."

Merl frowned. "I appreciate your bravery, but we can't afford to lose you."

"You won't," I promised.

Merl reluctantly agreed, as did Lenox. I sent up a small prayer that I would not let them down. Words from the Gita floated into my mind...*it is nature that causes all movement. Deluded by the ego, the fool harbors the perception that says "I did it".*

I could not let them down. But I could fail. And I could die.

CHAPTER ELEVEN
HOME AWAY FROM HOME

Sydney

The blades kicked up clouds of dust, and I had to cover my eyes as we ran away from the helicopter. Robert's hand on my elbow steered me through the darkness behind my lids. Blue's nose tapping my hip let me know he was by my side.

The sound of the blades receded, and I opened my eyes. The sun slid down the west side of the world, attaching long, dark shadows to the boulders around us.

Robert led me along a sandy path and around a bend where a small cabin, the same color as the landscape, sat against the rocks. Next to it a camouflaged tarp covered what looked like a motorcycle.

The fact that Robert had safe houses in the desert didn't surprise me. It *did* surprise me that when he opened the door it revealed an adorable space rather than something stark and primitive.

There were curtains on the windows, a queen-sized bed with a thick comforter, and a small kitchen, the shelves lined with canned foods.

Robert moved into the cabin, sitting down on one of the two chairs at the tiny kitchen table to untie his boots. "It's best not to wear shoes in here," he said. "Gets dirty really fast." He gestured with his chin toward the open door. "Sand tracks in." His eyes fell on Blue and he frowned. "Of course with that guy in here, taking off our shoes is almost pointless."

"Well, we won't be here long," I said. "We wanna get moving immediately don't we? Find her."

"No."

"What do you mean?"

"We're not gonna run out of here. We need to rest, pack our supplies. This isn't gonna be one of your charging-off-into-the-sunset-wanting-to-die-moments, Sydney." His eyes found mine, and they were hard. He wasn't going to be argued with. He wasn't going to do what I wanted...until he was good and ready.

"Fair enough. But, I'll point out that I have no intention of dying."

I sat on the other chair and began to untie my own laces.

Robert, in socked feet, went over to the kitchen sink to wash his hands.

"There's an outhouse through there." He gestured with his chin toward a door in the back wall of the cabin. "We'll sleep here tonight and head out in the morning. It gets really hot during the day, so I suggest we leave before the sun rises and then rest during the height of the heat."

"How far a walk is it from here?"

"Shouldn't take more than a day."

"We couldn't get dropped off any closer?" I wanted to find this woman, resolve this.

"No. We couldn't get dropped off closer. Don't be ridiculous."

"Why is that ridiculous?" I asked, kicking off my boots.

"You just—" Robert turned to me, drying his hands on a dish towel and leaning against the kitchen counter. "You just want everything to be your way."

I laughed. A good belly laugh. "You're one to talk. I never met a man who gets his way as much as you."

His eyes heated with anger. "You always get your way with me."

"Really? I do?"

"Yes." He turned back to the kitchen and started pulling down cans of beans.

"It seems like you're forgetting our very first argument."

"When I killed your brother's murderer. Did you a favor that you have held against me for years." He didn't turn around, but his voice was flat again, and I could guess that his expression had stilled. "Is that why you want to kill me?"

"He was mine to destroy. You stole that from me."

Robert began to open a can of beans. "I didn't steal anything from you. I did you a favor. Besides, that was eons ago. Since then, I've saved your life numerous times. I funded your vigilante network. I've done everything I could. Everything in my power to show you how much ..."

He didn't finish the sentence.

The can popped open and he lifted the lid, reaching for another can.

"I'd say 9 out of 10 times that you saved my ass it was really your ass that you were saving." I countered. "You're the most selfish human being on the planet. The only reason you help anyone is because you think it will help you."

"That's not true." He turned back to me, his mouth a grim line.

"Yes, it is. You destroyed the company that you built in order to make a shit ton of money. Also, so that you wouldn't have to face Joyful Justice anymore. You needed to change your ways, or you were going to get fucked by us."

A small smile pulled at the edge of his mouth. "I did it all for you, Sydney."

"That's another thing that's for you. Thinking you're doing it for me. Seriously, I bet if you ask any of your ex-wives—anyone you've ever worked with and they weren't afraid you'd kill them—they'd tell you that you're the most selfish man on the planet."

His eyes narrowed, and he crossed his arms...his hands close to his pistol. My body tensed. Robert Maxim was a dangerous man. His selfishness was part of his power. If you don't care about anyone but yourself, decisions become simple. Easy. Whereas when you're trying to help others, suddenly you have to weigh options. Have to weigh who will get hurt.

"You think I'm the most selfish man on the planet? You're the most selfish woman."

I shook my head. "I doubt it. But I'm not perfect."

He tipped his head back and laughed. His Adam's apple bobbing up and down.

"What's so funny?"

"Look at us," he said. "You and me, the most selfish people in the world. On a mission to go find a prophet from God. And what? Kill her?"

His gaze found mine. His blue-green eyes were bright with humor.

"Depends on what she has to say for herself," I said.

He laughed again. "You'd kill the woman who is freeing your sex from oppression."

"Is that what she's doing?"

"There is a revolution happening. There are women standing up and fighting against men for the first time ever."

"Not for the first time ever. Suffragettes and their kind have existed forever," I said, waving my hand at him. Just like Robert Maxim to ignore the value of the women's movement of the past several centuries.

"Here's the difference. These women are doing it for God. Do you know how much more powerful that is?"

I rolled my shoulders, not wanting to think too hard on it.

"When you do something for God, it's much more powerful than doing it for yourself, or your children, or your sisters." His voice dripped with condescension. Robert didn't have much respect for faith. "When you do it for God, you're doing it for so much more. It gives you a purpose. It gives your life value. That's why all these motherfuckers do this." Robert waived his arm around us, encompassing all motherfuckers who did anything. "All these Isis idiots, those crazy Christians holding "God hates fags" signs at military funerals. They're all doing it because they want their lives to have meaning."

"That sounds kind of selfish," I said with a smile.

Robert laughed again and turned back to his beans.

"Maybe it is selfish. But I think it's powerful. I think the woman we're going to find is incredibly powerful. Incredibly smart. And the most dangerous person on the planet right now."

A shiver ran up my spine. Robert Maxim was often right. What if I destroyed someone who could save us all just because I was selfish?

ƎK

Robert

I woke up with a jolt. Blue sat at the end of the bed, his ears perked, watching me. Sydney was on her side, curled away from me. The cabin was dark, the moonlight filtering in from outside pale—it was a new moon.

I'd been here on nights when the moon was full, and it practically looked like daylight outside. Tonight was the kind of night to stare at stars.

I had fallen asleep hard and fast. Exhaustion flooding over me and sinking me down so quickly that I hardly had a moment to enjoy the fact that I was in a bed with Sydney Rye.

I rolled toward her, staring at the back of her head. Blue watched me. If I touched her, he would stop me.

What had woken me? And why was Blue awake?

I listened closely but didn't hear anything. Getting out of the bed, I checked my phone. There was a message from Deacon.

The eagle is aware. Time to move on.

Martha knew.

The message had just arrived, but I had no idea how much time we had. Martha must have sent a team after me. Did she know the location of the safe house? It was possible.

I looked back over at the bed. Sydney's face was soft in sleep, her features mellowed, and the hard line of her brow smooth.

Her body was a series of soft curves. She looked more womanly, more feminine, in sleep. While awake and in action, there was a masculine edge to her. Or at least what society called a masculine edge.

I'd seen more and more of that type of movement since the Her

Prophet arrived on the scene. There was a way that women were walking now--that they didn't believe the centuries, the millennia of proof that they were the weaker sex. They were starting to realize how much power they held.

A shiver ran over me. What if all women were like Sydney Rye? Where would that leave the world?

It was ridiculous. There were few people as violent or cunning as her. No amount of belief in a prophet would change that.

But it could change a lot.

"Sydney," I whispered softly. Her eyes flicked open and found me in the darkness where I stood a few feet away at the table. "We need to move."

She sat up quickly and her eyes went to Blue. He stepped to her side.

I packed our bags, adding freeze-dried food, water purification tablets and sunscreen. I'd fashioned a pack for Blue so that he could carry supplies as well. We'd take my motorcycle as far as possible then trek the rest of the way. We'd be going slowly enough on this rough terrain for Blue to follow the bike.

Stepping outside as Sydney tied on her boots, I pulled the cover off my motorcycle, an all-black Ducati that I had fitted with specialty tires for the desert terrain. I ran my hand over its curves. It was like a woman. Like a tough, fast woman. My favorite kind.

The desert night was cold, and I turned up the collar of my jacket against its icy fingers. Sydney and Blue stepped out of the cabin as I stashed the packs.

"The bike can carry everything for now. But I've made a backpack for Blue too."

"That's smart." Sydney's voice was quiet.

I looked up at her, raising my brows. "What's up?"

"Nothing." But she didn't sound like herself. Was she about to fall under another influence? Was I about to lose Sydney Rye? What if it happened on the bike and she tried to kill me?

"Sydney." I walked up to her and took her by the shoulders, staring into her eyes. Her dark gray irises glinted up at me. "What am I gonna do if you lose it? If you try and kill me?"

Her lips curled up in a predatory smile. "You could let me drive." She gave a small shrug. "That way you know where my hands are. And like I said, I'm not suicidal."

"You're not suicidal. But who knows what the prophet did to you. Who knows what she planted in that brain of yours." I searched her face. Trying to find some evidence, some clue…but there was nothing there. Just the scars, the fine lines of aging, and the bright eyes of the woman I loved.

I'd die for her. I'd even let her drive my Ducati.

"Just to prove to you I'm not selfish, I'll let you drive."

"That doesn't prove you're not selfish, Robert. If you're letting me drive so that you can be sure I won't murder you, then it's totally selfish. You see my point?" She raised her eyebrows at me.

I laughed. "I don't think that's the case. I'm letting you drive my bike because I think you'll enjoy it. And I want you to be happy."

It was her turn to laugh. "You want me to be happy? Wow. Is that a thing? Happiness?"

I shrugged and gestured for her to get on the bike first. "You tell me after you handle this beauty."

Her eyes ran over the bike like a man ogling a hot woman on the street. "Oh, you're right; this is gonna be fun."

It wasn't my favorite fantasy about Sydney Rye, but riding behind her on a motorcycle was definitely up there on the visualization board of Robert Maxim. My thighs cupping her ass, my hands around her taut waist. The way she concentrated on the path ahead, following my directions as I navigated through the rugged landscape.

We didn't go fast, but it saved our strength for the journey ahead.

Every time I glanced back, I found Blue behind us, his white fur lit by the pale moon as he jogged to keep up.

Where did his loyalties lie? He was devoted to Sydney. But he also must be devoted to his puppies. And he let Sydney be controlled by the prophet. Why would Blue do that?

Which side was he on?

EK

Sydney

I liked this bike. It handled well, and the strong rumble of the engine sent a thrill of power up my spine.

Lightning sizzled at the edge of my vision—easy to distinguish from reality. The pale light of the moon illuminated the path and Robert's body behind mine kept away the chill.

As we moved further away from the cabin, I grew calmer. *I was on the right path.* I needed to find *Her*. What I did once I got there would come to me.

The distant thwop of a helicopter rose over the growl of the engine.

Robert pointed to our left to a large boulder.

"Quickly, stop over there. They're here."

I pulled into the shadow of the boulder and Maxim climbed off. Blue raced up to us and Robert signaled for us all to crouch down, hiding in the boulder's dark shadow. The helicopter's bright beam focused over the cabin several miles away. It backtracked and landed in the same spot that Deacon had chosen hours earlier.

Robert's breath brushed my cheek as we huddled at the edge of the boulder, watching through Robert's binoculars as armed men ran from the helicopter into the cabin.

"How did they find us?" I asked.

"They're the CIA, Sydney. They have their ways."

"You think one of your men gave up this location?"

"It's possible. But don't worry, I'm prepared."

"Of course you are." A smile tugged at my lips. I did appreciate how Robert Maxim was always prepared.

The men came back out and climbed into the helicopter. It took off and circled the cabin. The light landed on our tracks and they began to follow the motorcycle's trail. "Shit," Maxim said before turning to the bike. He opened up a side compartment and pulled out an Uzi. "I don't want to have to kill any of them."

"'Cause we're kind of on the same side?" I asked.

"They're just men following orders. Men I've probably worked with."

"But you're willing to kill them?" I asked.

"They're not taking you anywhere," Robert said handing me a second Uzi.

"Maybe you should take the bike. Distract them," I said.

He shook his head. "No. They won't stop looking for you. They need to not find us."

The helicopter was getting closer. My grip on the gun tightened. Blue growled low in his throat.

The wind from the blades kicked up sand, spiraling it into the bright beam of their searchlight. What would a machine gun do against a helicopter? We'd have to wait for the men to descend. And then kill them.

They probably weren't trying to kill us, though. "Do you think they just want to talk?" I asked Robert.

"Yes. Talk," Robert said, his voice quiet.

"Then we shouldn't kill them. Let them take me for an interrogation."

"You'll never get out again, Sydney. If Martha doesn't outright kill you, she'll put you in a black ops prison for the rest of your days. You can either die here tonight, or die after they've tortured you for all the information they can get."

Well, when he put it that way...

A whistling sound pierced the night, and suddenly a missile of some kind impacted with the helicopter. It twisted out of the air, igniting into flame, a bloom of black smoke billowing into the dark sky as it tilted and plummeted toward the ground. The horrendous wrenching of metal crashing into rock blasted through the night.

I started running back down the path toward the crashed helicopter, Blue by my side. The glow of the fire lit up the night but the wreckage was hidden behind other boulders.

"What are you doing?" Robert called as he followed me.

"They might need our help," I yelled.

"Need our help! We were about to kill them."

"Yeah, but we didn't want to."

As we came around a bend the wreckage appeared; the helicopter lay crumpled on its side, the windshield shattered. A body slumped in the pilot seat. But the co-pilot crawled, dragging broken legs behind him, trying to get away from the burning fuselage.

I ran to him even as Robert yelled behind me. "It's going to blow; don't be an idiot!"

I grabbed the man's arm and suddenly Robert was there, grabbing his other side. We dragged him back up the path, toward our hiding place, away from the dangers of the imminent explosion.

The earth shook, and the night sky lit up as the helicopter's fuel tank caught. Robert and I were knocked to the ground, the heat searing. I scrambled to stand, grabbed the soldier again, and with Robert's help we took shelter behind a boulder.

The man groaned as we laid him down.

"There are enemy combatants out there, Sydney. We don't know how many. We don't know where they are. But they certainly know we're here now."

Robert was right. But I couldn't just leave this man to die. "Please," he whispered. "My legs."

I looked down at them. And my vision flashed back to Mulberry lying on the battlefield. This man still had his legs, but they were broken, twisted at horrific angles.

What could I do?

The man reached for a radio on his chest and talked into it. "Copter down. Under enemy fire." The crackle and spit of the radio joined with the thunder in my mind.

My gaze traveled to the hilltops above us—dark figures appeared out of the night. We were surrounded.

CHAPTER TWELVE
LOVE IS A BATTLEFIELD

Anita

The light from my computer screen cast a blue flickering glow over the living room. London in February was wet, cold, and dark. The sun, which had only managed to cast a dull gray gloom into the room, had set and now darkness encompassed the space.

Huddled under a blanket, a glass of red wine in my hand, I'd started watching videos of the Butcher after reading Lenox's update; Mulberry had started physical therapy, and Lenox still couldn't reach Sydney or Bobby.

I'd also checked #IAmHer and found the numbers even higher—it felt like a tsunami was about to be upon us, and now was when the ocean was pulling back, gathering for the giant wave that would wash everything away.

I'd set up meetings with several friends who'd known Rida, so I had nothing to do now but wait.

My melancholy had drawn me to the Butcher's videos. Over 6'5", broad, a former Iraqi soldier in Saddam's army, he'd earned the name the Butcher two years prior.

In all of the videos, he stood on a stage, his trademark machete in hand, a woman at his feet, her face and hair exposed, her body at his mercy. A crowd cheering him on. How many in that crowd could do what the Butcher did? Could exact the justice for which they screamed?

What percentage of the population could actually *do it*?

Had I always had it in me to kill? Or was it my life on the line, the repeated violation of my body, that let me strangle my captor to death?

I pulled the blanket around me tighter, the wet chill of London creeping in on me. Putting down my glass of red wine, I closed the computer. I needed to take a break.

The darkness settled in, and I blinked against it, my eyes slowly adjusting. It was a small space, with modern furniture and sleek lines. Apparently, Sydney had owned the apartment when she worked here as a private eye, and Joyful Justice had decided to keep it.

I didn't know much about Sydney's history. The few things we'd spoken about in the time we spent together had been vague. She was the center of so many people's lives. But in her apartment there wasn't a single photo, no knick-knacks, nothing personal at all.

The one thing I'd seen that could be remotely considered personal was a dog dish with Blue's name on it. But that could've been a gift. A small smile crossed my lips as I pictured Mulberry giving it to her, trying to make her life homey.

I pushed off the blanket and stood, clicking on a lamp. I needed to order some food, get out of this funk. Get out of my head.

Waiting for Zerzan or anyone else to drop the video felt like torture. Part of me wanted to do it myself just to stop the anticipation. I made my way into the kitchen and pulled out the takeout menus. A good London curry was what I needed. Something nostalgic.

The years I'd spent in this city had been some of the best of my life. I'd been young, eager to learn, excited to be out from under the watchful eye of my family and neighbors.

London was so different from India. And not just that it had wet, cold weather, but that women had a standing here they didn't have in my home country. When Tom and I went on our first date, the waiter turned to me when it was time to order. In India, no waiter ever asked the woman what she wanted. They only addressed the man of the table.

I became flummoxed, heat racing to my cheeks. And Tom answered for me. We had discussed what we each wanted to order, the way couples do.

After the waiter left, he'd apologized. *Apologized for ordering for me.*

I'd brushed it off, saying that I'd had something stuck in my throat and drinking quickly from my water glass.

I should've never married him.

I put aside the takeout menus as my appetite fled, the memories of our brief life together overpowering my mind. Our little flat, the way I woke up in the morning to him watching me sleep. He pushed my hair behind my ear and told me I was beautiful and that he loved me.

Queasiness swamped me. I didn't deserve his love. I never did.

A knock at the door sent fear racing through my veins. *Who could it be?*

I grabbed a knife from the butcher block on the counter and approached the front door on socked feet, quiet and ready to defend myself, relieved I'd pushed the deadbolt into place.

I looked out the peephole and my mouth went completely dry.

It was Tom.

How did he find me?

It must've been my friend, Angela. She'd asked where I was staying, and I'd told her—thinking we might meet for a drink here but then she'd suggested a bar. She'd always been friends with Tom. Had she asked my address just to pass on the information?

Tom chewed on his bottom lip before reaching up and knocking again. Looking around the hall, a line of frustration formed between his eyebrows.

I hadn't seen him in two years, and now I drank him in, basking in the blue green of his eyes, in his tangles of brown hair.

He turned to leave, and my hand undid the bolt as my eye stayed pressed to the hole. He turned back at the sound, his eyebrows rising and hope sparking in his gaze.

I stepped back and opened the door, keeping the knife behind my thigh.

His breath caught and his eyes found mine. "I'll leave if you want. Just nod and I'll walk away," he said.

My heart ached. *He thought I didn't want him.* Couldn't understand that I didn't deserve him. That I never did.

We stared at each other. I couldn't answer.

His smell drifted around me.

His black raincoat was dotted with raindrops, the umbrella in his hand dripping silently onto the carpeted hall floor. The smell of London rain wafted off of him: the chalky scent of wet cement and the sweet, cloying perfume of diesel.

He stepped forward slightly, grasping the umbrella in both hands now. "Can I come in, then?"

"Yes," I said. The same word I used when he proposed marriage. The same word I used when he asked if I was leaving him. The same word I used now, letting him back into my life.

Yes.

EK

Tom stepped forward as I stepped back, and I pressed myself against the wall, letting him pass, keeping the knife hidden behind my thigh. He moved into the apartment and stopped before entering the living room.

"Where should I put my umbrella?"

"I don't know."

I didn't know anything. Why did I let him in? Why was he here? We stared at each other, the umbrella dripping onto the floor.

"Angela told me you were here."

I nodded.

"You never responded to any of my calls, any of my texts." A line of frustration reappeared between his brows. I was too frustrating. Too set in my ways. Too ambitious to be a wife. *I had to be on my own.*

But look where that got me. Where was I now? Not where I thought I'd be. But doing more than I ever thought I could. *I still couldn't be with Tom.*

I still couldn't be happy, peaceful. Not when there was so much injustice in the world.

I hardened the wall around my heart. I made sure to tell my body not to respond to him. Nothing had changed about *us*, even if everything else had.

"Will you..." Tom didn't finish the sentence. He ran a wet hand through his hair. The curls bounced back up, they were impossible to tame. *Like me.*

Poor Tom.

"Look, I understand you've been gone. I understand you had work you wanted to do. I just...how could you just cut me out of your life?"

"I had to." My voice came out quiet and unsure.

"Why?" His tone was a mix of anger and curiosity.

He'd never understood. How could he? A white, Englishman. How could he understand what an Indian woman needed? How I had to free myself to find myself?

His mother's words floated through my mind. *You're very pretty for an Indian girl...* She'd said it the first time we met, and I'd thought she was a bitch. Hadn't realized that all I'd ever be in Tom's world was an *Indian girl*. Never an equal...always an "other", an outsider. *I didn't need them.*

"I'm sorry, Tom. I don't know what else we have to say to each other."

"Will you..." He had a question he wasn't asking. "I'm sorry for whatever I did."

"I told you." I looked down at my feet. "It was about *me* Tom, never about you." A cliché break-up line that in this case was true. I forced my gaze to meet his. To try to *make* him understand. *I didn't want to be in his world.*

His mouth parted, eyes pleading.

I needed a drink.

"Do you want a glass of wine?"

"Yes, please." He gave a short laugh. It came out harder than his normal laugh. Tom's real laugh was one of those great things, a sound that always brought a flutter to my chest, made me want to grab and kiss him.

He shrugged out of his jacket and hung it on a hook in the hall, leaning his umbrella beneath it. I moved past him into the small kitchen and stashed the knife before pulling down another glass, and pouring him wine with an unsteady hand.

I looked up at him to see his gaze on the tremor in my fingers. I put the bottle back securely onto the counter. When I passed him the glass, my hand stayed steady.

He wrapped his fingers around it and my own hand.

"You look beautiful," Tom said, his voice low, quiet. *Authentic.*

I turned away from him, and he let my hand slip out from underneath his. He never tried to make me do anything I didn't want to do. It wasn't that he was some controlling patriarchal man. It was that I needed to stand on my own two feet.

I couldn't be in a partnership. He deserved better.

But I was, wasn't I? I partnered with Dan, Merl, Lenox, Sydney...we all worked together. Our unity gave us strength.

But, Tom and I could never be together again. I couldn't tell him about Joyful Justice. He was a freaking barrister—an officer of the court.

"So, what brings you back to London?" Tom asked, leaning against the counter of the narrow, galley kitchen.

He was wearing a suit, so he must've just come from work. His tie had come a little loose, and I stared at the top button of his shirt. I wanted to unbutton it. Run my fingers over his collarbone. Kiss his lips and melt into him. Let him carry some of my burden.

But if I put it down, would I be strong enough to pick it up again?

"I'm looking up an old friend. For a story."

"Where are you working these days?" He asked.

"Freelancing still."

"Your article about Kalpesh was amazing." He sipped his wine.

I had written it after Sydney saved me. In the story I didn't talk about my own capture, my own rape and torture. But I did expose the monster who orchestrated it, Kalpesh Khan. I exposed other victims' stories. *Too much of a coward to expose my own.*

"Thank you," I said.

"What is it?" He cocked his head at me. I turned and grabbed another glass, pouring myself wine and taking a sip before answering.

"Nothing, just tired. I just got in today."

"From where? Where are you living?"

He sounded eager. He wanted every detail. He wanted to know me again.

Could I let him?

No.

"I spend most of my time in New York," I lied.

"Do you like America?" He sipped his wine.

"Yes, I think it's fine."

"So what's the story? What are you working on?"

"It's about the new prophet. The Her Prophet."

His eyebrows rose. "I've heard rumors...I'm sure you're the perfect person to tell that story."

I would be the one manipulating it.

"Well, we'll see."

"So who are you looking up?"

"Do you remember Rida?" Tom had met her dozens of times. She'd attended our wedding, but so had a couple hundred others, so if he couldn't remember Rida it wasn't exactly insulting.

"Of course I do. Shy, sweet, brilliant as far as I can recall."

"Yes, she's Syrian. I think she might be able to help me with some information I need." I wanted to steer him away from me. I didn't want to lie to him anymore. "What are you working on?" I asked.

"Same old, same old." He shrugged. "Trying to save the world." He gave me a wry smile. Tom worked as a human rights attorney and was damn good.

"And you're still living in the city obviously," I said.

Tom nodded and sucked his lower lip between his teeth, watching me. I couldn't look at him when he did that. This is why I had stayed away. He had too much power over me.

"Why didn't you ever respond to any of my calls or texts?" he asked.

I turned to the sink and busied myself washing a water glass I'd used earlier. It was easier to talk to him when I wasn't looking at him. "I just needed it to end. It was much harder if we were still speaking."

"I think I let you go too easily."

Tears sprung unwelcome to my eyes, burning, pushing to be released.

"I asked you to let me go," I said.

He shifted closer to me. The glass was clean, but I kept scrubbing it.

"But, Anita, did you really stop loving me?"

A lump in my throat blocked me from answering. *Of course not. I never stopped loving him. I just couldn't be with him then. I had to...*

I couldn't be married to a barrister.

"I'm sorry Tom. I didn't want to hurt you." My voice came out tight. I obviously sounded like I was on the verge of tears.

His hand landed on my shoulder, and I wanted to recoil, but instead I leaned into his touch. I put the glass on the sideboard and turned off the water. Grasping onto the edge of the sink I kept myself from turning into his embrace.

"Anita, I've never stopped loving you. I'd do anything to get you back. I'm ready to fight."

"I'm not." I had to dash at tears escaping from my eyes before I could continue. "I'm not the same woman you were married to. I've changed a lot."

"I love you unconditionally, Anita. I always have. I don't love any specific act or way that you are. I love *you*. All of you. As you've always been and you always will be."

He was too good. Too sweet. Too supportive.

"Please." I don't know what I was asking for. For him to go away. For him to force me into an embrace. For him to just keep standing there forever.

"I'm sorry." His arm traveled down my shoulder blade and wrapped around my bicep, giving a small pull. "Now that I see you again, I can't just let you go. I can't just let you out of my life without trying. Begging. Fighting for you to be mine again."

He tugged a little harder, and I fell against his chest. His smell engulfed me as his arms wrapped around my body and the tears came, hot and heavy and ugly. I shook with the force of them. Tom rubbed my back and whispered into my ear that he loved me.

He was holding me up. I was falling and he was catching me. How would I stand on my own ever again?

His arm wrapped around my waist and pulled me closer. I fit into the shelter of his body, my arms around him and squeezing, feeling the hard planes of his chest through his dress shirt. He smelled like Tom; London rain and Sandalwood, with just a hint of clean soap. "Anita, Anita, Anita," he whispered, kissing the top of my head, nuzzling my hair. "I'm here; you don't need to worry anymore."

It was too easy. He made me feel too safe. *I couldn't let it fool me.*

I pushed back from him, but his arms stayed tight.

"Please," he whispered against my hair. "Please let me help you."

But there was no way for him to help me. Only *I* could help me.

"Please let me go." My voice came out quiet, thick with tears.

"I refuse to let you go again." His voice had a hard edge to it—an edge I'd never heard from him before.

We'd had only a year of being married, six months of which I'd spent pulling away from him as I began to realize how much my life had become about his life. About his big career, about his successful family, about our future children. I'd realized I'd made a huge mistake. I couldn't be his wife then, and I couldn't let him hold me now.

I pushed against his chest, and he released me with a deep sigh. One of my shirt sleeves rode up as I stepped back from him, keeping my hands on his chest, and he looked down at my hands.

They were scarred with nicks from my life.

He grabbed my wrist, seeing the scars there from the shackles I'd worn during my imprisonment. His eyes went round and his lips turned into a deep frown.

"Anita, what happened to you?" Anger bubbled in his voice. He was gonna try and solve that, too.

"I was held prisoner." I couldn't believe I said it out loud. And it didn't even hurt. I hadn't told anyone—except for Dan, but, of course he knew. He was a part of rescuing me.

I'd saved myself, though. That's what Sydney said. She said that I saved myself, and that she and Dan just provided the getaway vehicle.

Though without a getaway vehicle, I probably would have died.

121

Killing my guard, strangling him to death with the chains that he bound me with, would not have freed me without Sydney arriving to remove those chains, help me through the maze-like mansion, and get me into the van waiting to take me away.

"You what?" Tom asked, his eyes flicking up to mine.

"I was a prisoner." My voice sounded hard, as hard as the iron manacles that left the scars on my wrists.

He pushed up my sleeve further, seeing the round burns from the cigarettes they'd ground into my flesh. A sheen stole over his eyes as his other hand came to my wrist, his thumb running over the puckered marks.

"Someone burned you with cigarettes?" His voice was a low growl. He reminded me of Blue in that moment. Of an animal, incapable of clear thoughts, running only on instinct.

"Yes."

"And did they…" He paused, his gaze finding mine again, and the question remained unasked. *Did they rape you?*

"Yes," I answered, firming my voice. *I would not cry.* I would not cry as those memories flooded back, as my body tensed with the trauma of what had happened to me.

"My God." His eyes welled with tears.

I tried to pull away from him; his sympathy was devastating. I didn't need it. And I didn't want it.

"Anita." His voice was edged with that anger again. My eyes flicked back to his—the same rich green as fir trees, with flecks of bark brown. The trees that covered his family's estate outside of London.

I'd left him so that I could become me. So that I could become this powerful woman: saving others, using my skills and my heart to free the world from patriarchy and violence.

"Tom." I put ice into my voice—let it chill right down my throat, building an ice dam around my heart.

It was the only way to stay safe.

He stepped forward, my wrist still in his hand, and pulled me against his chest, laying my palm against his cheek. I could feel rough stubble there. He hadn't shaved since morning. Had come here straight from work.

"Anita, I understand why you left me."

That was impossible. A white man from a rich family could never understand why I'd had to go.

He'd had the best of intentions. Always treated me as an equal. Always wanted me to be happy. But that, in and of itself, was a cage. I was a prisoner of his status. Even if he didn't see me that way, the world did.

"Tom, I think you should go." He moved quickly, so fast that my breath caught in my throat. And then his lips were on mine, forceful and urgent and demanding.

I was his, and he wasn't going to let me go this time.

My defenses shuddered at the brush of his lips, at the warmth of his tongue, at the insistence of his love.

He pushed me back against the counter in that small galley kitchen, and I wrapped my arms around his neck and melted against him, the ice dam I'd built up in my chest flooding away.

This time I wasn't crying; this time I was yielding. It was the first time I'd been kissed since the assault, and it felt so damn good. Tom wasn't trying to take anything from me. He was trying to be with me. *He loved me.*

And maybe just for tonight I could let him. Maybe just this once. I wasn't gonna go back to him, but I needed this.

Wasn't a part of standing on your own two feet taking what you needed?

I heard pinging. My phone was pinging. And I didn't care.

My leg rode up and wrapped around his hip, and he groaned, pushing himself against me. His hands dove under my shirt and slid up the silky sides of me, up my ribcage, holding me there, one hand on either side as he kissed me. And kissed me. And kissed me.

But that pinging didn't stop. My phone was going nuts.

And through the fog of lust and freedom and want, I realized something massive was happening.

I pulled away from him, raising my mouth so that I could breathe, and he kissed my chin, my throat, down to my collarbones, licking the hollow between them.

I put my hands on his shoulders, steadying myself. I wanted him. I wanted this night, free of any entanglements. Just a trustworthy partner. Someone who would fight for me. Someone who needed me. Someone whose strength I could take, knowing he had plenty to give.

But my phone. My phone kept pinging.

I took a hand off his shoulder to reach out and grab it off the counter. Alerts. Alerts from Twitter, from Facebook. Three texts from Dan.

Oh, shit. The video had gone live.

EK

Mulberry

I shifted my weight, bringing my legs around so that I was sitting on the edge of the bed. Gripping my jaw, I eyed the wheel chair. *I could do this.* Sweat dripped over my brow, stinging my eyes. I swiped at it and glanced up at my physical therapist.

Onder nodded, encouraging me. "You've got this."

I sucked in a deep breath and reached out to the wheelchair, using my upper body to maneuver myself into it. My arm muscles shook with the effort. "Breathe," Onder reminded me.

Fuck you. My breath came out in a whoosh as I dropped into the chair, my whole body trembling.

Onder's hand landed on my shoulder and squeezed. "Great job, Mulberry."

"It's ridiculous. I never needed—" I shook my head, not finishing the sentence. My upper body had always been strong. Even as a teenager, I'd been effortlessly muscular and physically capable. To find myself a divorced, middle-aged man, missing a limb, who could barely maneuver himself into a wheelchair, was almost as painful as the throbbing nerve endings in my stump.

"Onder," I said. "Tell me again how long until I get a prosthetic?"

This phase needed to be over. I needed to be walking. I needed my life back.

"Soon. You're doing great."

"Yeah, great," I said.

There was a knock at the door, and Lenox came in. His lean body moved effortlessly— broad shoulders, narrow waist, *two* legs...if I didn't like him so much I'd have to hate him. "Looking good," he said, gesturing to the wheelchair.

"Am I?"

Lenox grinned, his teeth flashing. "Sitting up, moving around. Not just lying in your bed like a sack of potatoes. Yeah, I'd say you're looking good."

I winced. Days ago I'd been unconscious. Now, at least I was a conscious sack of potatoes. This sack of potatoes could move itself into a wheelchair. *The little things.*

"I've got some news that's going cheer you up," Lenox said in his lilting accent as he moved into the room.

"Oh, yeah?"

"Yeah," he nodded. "Sandy just got off the plane. She will be here soon."

My heart started to hammer in my chest. *Sandy.* I couldn't wait to see her. *How did I ever lose her?*

The loss of Sandy and my marriage hurt...and felt unreal. Like my leg, the ghost of it still lingered—my brain refused to believe it was gone.

What had happened between us? Hours combing through my memories had revealed no clue as to the last ten years—the last thing I could remember was leaving the house for work. Saying goodbye to Sandy, giving her a kiss, and she turned her cheek away, angry at me for something but I didn't think it would lead to this: a separation, a divorce.

Neither of us even *believed* in divorce. Both from Catholic families, when we said we were gonna stick it out forever, we'd meant it.

But I guess we didn't.

However, the fact that Sandy was willing to fly across the world meant she wasn't totally lost to me.

"Onder, let's keep going."

"I think you've done enough for today. Get yourself back into your bed, and we can consider it a success."

"I'd rather see Sandy sitting up, if you don't mind. I think I'd look less like an invalid." I smiled. "What do you think, Lenox? Which looks better, in a hospital bed? Or in a wheelchair?" I barked a laugh.

Lenox laughed, too. "Hey, man, you look good either way."

Lenox was a friend. That much was clear. He'd refused to explain to me what we did, saying it was top secret. *Had I gone to work for the CIA? That didn't sound like me. Maybe an anti-terrorist unit within the NYPD.*

Lenox promised to tell me eventually, or I'd remember. In the meantime, I should concentrate on getting better. Concentrate on learning to walk again.

I hauled myself back into the bed, just for the practice, and lay there shaking, letting my eyes slide shut. I must have fallen asleep, because a soft knock at the door woke me.

I opened my eyes to see Sandy stepping into the room. She wore loose jeans and a white cable knit sweater. Her blonde hair was up in a ponytail. There were dark circles under her eyes and fine lines that hadn't been there the last time I'd seen her. My breath stuck in my throat as I took her in.

She was as beautiful as ever. *I loved her as much as ever.*

Her eyes filled with tears, and she put a hand to her lips sucking in a breath.

"Is it that bad?" I asked, bracing myself for the answer.

She shook her head, crossing the room to me, slowly, approaching me like I might be dangerous. Like I might hurt her. "It just brings back some pretty bad memories," she said, standing over me, her fingers twining together.

"Memories, funny you should mention those," I said, trying to make a joke about my amnesia. *Haha.* "Have a seat, please." I gestured to the chair next to my bed.

"I, yes, your friend told me," Sandy sat in the chair, her eyes holding mine. "You don't remember..."

"Baby," I reached and caught her hand, looking down at where my ring used to sit. *There wasn't even a tan line.* "Baby, what happened between us? I don't understand."

Tears welled in her eyes, and she squeezed my hand. "You never did beat around the bush," she said with a small smile, then looked down at our joined hands. "Mulberry, you...you were shot. Do you remember that?"

"I don't remember it but..."

She reached up and touched my shoulder where I had noticed a bullet scar but hadn't known when it happened.

"Ten years ago. You were working, and you were shot, and I was so scared. And I realized that I couldn't. I wasn't meant to be a policeman's wife." She pulled her lip between her teeth and bit down on it, staring at my shoulder, her eyes misted with memories.

"But, I don't understand." *That didn't make any sense.* Sandy had known what I was when we got married.

"It was losing the baby *and* that—I just couldn't take it."

The hairs on the back of my neck stood up, and ice crystallized in my veins. "Losing the baby?"

She pulled her hand from mine and covered her face. "I'm messing this up. I have to remember that you can't remember," she said into her hands.

"It's okay; go slow, I'm listening." Leaning over, I put my hand on her knee. She sobbed. I wanted to put my arms around her, climb out of the bed and pull her to me, but I couldn't. I was too weak. Anger sizzled through me, chasing away the ice of fear. *What the hell had happened? What the hell had I done?*

She sucked in a stuttering breath. "I was pregnant—when you were shot, I was pregnant. And I hadn't told you. And then you were shot, and I lost the baby."

I stared at her. We'd wanted children. Always talked about having lots of them. *Loads.*

Sandy came from a big family. And I'd always wanted one. "Oh," was all that I said. I wanted to say more. Wanted to say all the words that would take away the pain, take away the past and make her mine again. But I had no idea what they were, or if I had the strength to say them.

"I realized that I couldn't have a family with you. That I couldn't handle the stress. That we couldn't be together."

"I wasn't willing to give up the job for you," I said, my voice a monotone. *Of course not.* The anger mellowed into a numbing warmth. *It was important to do the greater good; sacrifice was the highest honor.* The highest purpose.

I looked down at my leg…at where my leg used to be.

Had I sacrificed enough now? Could I give up throwing myself in front of others? And maybe, maybe Sandy would take me back?

CHAPTER THIRTEEN
THE STRANGER IN US ALL

Robert

My heart rate slowed as my vision sharpened. The scent of smoke and the flickering flames of the crashed helicopter calmed me.

Glancing at Sydney, her face all hard angles and determined lines, assured me she had control.

The shaggy hair and the black clothing of the figures approaching us meant they were Isis fighters.

The American soldier at our feet continued to yell into his radio, giving his location, and describing the situation, yelling to be heard over the crackling flames.

Fully surrounded.

Need support now.

Two men gone.

I recognized the soldier. I'd tried to hire him the year before—he turned me down. *Wanted to serve his country.* If he'd come to work for me, he wouldn't be about to die.

They'd only sent three people after us. Martha expected us to come easy. She didn't think that I would be willing to risk my company, my reputation, my life. She had severely underestimated my devotion to Sydney Rye.

I began to back up, headed toward the motorcycle, but keeping my eyes on the fighters arrayed above us.

One jumped down, landing on a nearby boulder.

Sydney bent down and grabbed the soldier by the back of his flak jacket, beginning to haul him along. Blue stayed by her side, a low growl emanating from his chest, his lip hovering above his teeth—they glistened in the flames, light, sharp and deadly.

The other Isis fighters began climbing down, and so instead of arguing with Sydney about how the injured soldier's dead weight would kill us, I grabbed his other arm and helped.

We navigated down the narrow passage toward the motorcycle and its hiding place. I had more weapons there. The niche between two boulders, up against a tall cliff face, provided decent cover.

Isis's recent defeats had pushed them into this desolate land, shrinking their territory and leaving them hungry for a victory. We must look like an easy prize.

They couldn't imagine what they actually faced.

A bullet exploded against a boulder to our right, and more sank into the sand at our feet. *Their attack had begun.* Debris sliced my cheek, and I flinched but kept moving.

Reaching the motorcycle, we dropped the American, and, after retreating into the niche, Sydney turned back to face the narrow opening. Dropping down on one knee, she brought the machine gun up and fired, the expulsion of the bullets shaking her thin form.

Blue sat behind her, his attention riveted to the American...his charge.

I grabbed supplies from the bike: several grenades and a sniper rifle. Then I began to scale the boulder next to us.

Sydney continued to fire as I climbed. I'd counted ten Isis soldiers, but there could be more coming.

Reaching the top of the boulder, I set up my sniper rifle, placing my grenades next to me. Lying flat on my stomach, creating as low a profile as possible, I searched the darkness. The fighters' black clothing blended with the night, but the fire from their weapons gave away their locations.

I zeroed in on my first target. His shaggy head arched back as a bullet entered his brain.

The rat-tat-tat of Sydney's gun silenced for a moment as she reloaded. An Isis soldier ran full bore—taking her silence as an opportunity to attack. I hit him in the shoulder, and his body twisted so I could aim at his face. I ended him.

The staccato of Sydney's gun started up again. Two more men came down the path, clearly willing to die in this battle, thinking they had somewhere to go.

Sydney and I knew this was it for us. *There is no afterlife, only this one.*

I took the pin out of a grenade and tossed it behind the approaching soldiers. Its explosion sent rock and sand into the air, throwing the two combatants forward.

Rocks tumbled down the slope onto the path, creating an additional barricade between the rest of the soldiers and us. They had to climb over the rubble, exposing themselves to my sniper fire.

The two fighters who had fallen scrambled to their feet but fell again under Sydney's fire.

No more Isis men appeared. *Not complete idiots or totally suicidal.* But also not our only concern.

The American soldier Sydney insisted on saving had contacted his base, so backup would arrive. While they could take out the Isis fighters, they would also want to take Sydney away.

We had to move soon.

I pressed my eye to the sniper rifle scope, scanning the area.

"Robert, above you!" Sydney yelled. I rolled onto my back just as an Isis soldier fell onto me.

A knife stabbed into my shoulder: painless at first, yet chilling. I grunted as it hit the bone, that sickening sound ringing through my body.

I brought up my hand gun, placing it to his temple. His skull shattered, and blood exploded over my face.

I rolled away, pushing him off to the side. His body thumped onto the rock, slid off and fell to the ground in front of the boulder.

A bullet hit the stone next to me. More men hung from the cliff face above. I grabbed my Uzi and sprayed, hitting the rock, pieces of it exploding off. The men fell with soft cries and landed with hard thumps.

The distant sound of a helicopter broke through the rush of blood in my ears.

We were running out of time.

"Sydney, we've got to get out of here."

She didn't respond. I glanced over the rock and saw her struggling, a soldier on top of her, Blue wrestling with another. The American passed out, possibly dead.

A knife glinted in the low light. I raised my weapon to kill her attacker, but a cry from above drew my attention. An Isis fighter fell through the air, having leapt from a dozen feet above me.

I stepped to the side, but he slammed into my shoulder, both of us falling off the boulder, spiraling through space.

The ground slammed into my back, knocking the wind out of me, and I rolled onto my side, finding my footing but realizing I'd lost my weapon.

We'd landed on the far side of the boulder, away from Sydney and Blue. The man who'd leapt on me rose to his feet.

Unlike most the soldiers, his face was clean-shaven...oh no, it wasn't that he'd shaved. *This was a boy.*

He ran at me, his eyes wild, his nose already bloodied from the fall.

I drew the pistol from my belt milliseconds before he rammed into me. But this time I only stepped back—he was light, a child, practically. *Shit.*

I raised my weapon, bringing it down onto the back of his head. He slumped against me, and I held him up for a moment before dropping him to the ground. My eyes couldn't leave his face. *So young.*

I raised my weapon, aiming it at his forehead. I should kill him, but something stilled my hand. *Pull the trigger*, I demanded of myself, but I just stood there staring at him.

Long, dark lashes against unlined skin, the dusting of a mustache on his top lip, his thin shoulders rising and falling gently with each breath.

I couldn't kill him.

EK

Sydney

The stink of him filled my nostrils as I sucked in a breath moments before he cut off my windpipe with one hand.

Blue wrestled with another man, the sounds of their struggle fading as my heartbeat filled my ears.

My gun, empty of bullets, lay pressed between me and my attacker.

Bearded, with long, matted hair, the Isis fighter's dark eyes stared into mine, his face close, and his breath on my cheek.

Raising himself up, Dark Eyes pressed his full weight against my throat, his mouth pulling into a frown of concentration. Stars danced across my vision as he pulled a blade from his belt.

By lifting his body to leverage his weight against my neck, Dark Eyes left my hands free. Fumbling, my fingers numb, I pulled out my own knife.

The rough-textured handle, the way it fit into my palm, brought me a surge of relief even as my lungs screamed for air. I stabbed up into the fighter's side with all my strength. Dark Eyes bent around the blade and grunted with pain, dropping his own knife but not releasing his hold on my neck.

More black spots.

I yanked the knife free and thrust it in again. Warm blood flowed over my hand as he whispered a string of curses yet maintained his hold on my throat.

My vision narrowed to a pinpoint.

I had to get him off me.

I brought the knife up again, this time slicing it along his forearm. Blood poured from the cut, racing down his arm to his fingers and my neck, but Dark Eyes' grip did not loosen.

Blue's bark joined the rushing of blood in my ears, and as my vision began to fade, Blue slammed into Dark Eyes, knocking him off me.

The man gave a terrified scream—they were up against the boulder, Blue's body over Dark Eyes, his teeth searching for the man's bearded neck.

I rolled onto my side, coughing, sucking in air, my knife still gripped in my hand.

I rose onto my knees as Blue found purchase on the man's throat. Dark Eyes struggled furiously, punching at Blue and thrashing beneath him. Blue bit down and yanked back, ripping open a wound in the man's neck. The fight drained out of him, and those dark eyes dimmed into nothingness.

The soft sound of footsteps behind me brought me to my feet, my knife up, knees bent.

Robert appeared from the other side of the boulder, his hair dusted in sand, his clothing disheveled, blood seeping from his shoulder. "Let's move," he said, striding past me toward the motorcycle, ignoring the bloodied body Blue still stood above.

I nodded, my throat raw.

Robert kneeled next to the American, checking his pulse. "Dead," he said, rising and moving to the motorcycle. He grabbed a pack off the bike, then pulled me toward the rocks. Blue leapt up after us, finding purchase with his nails and scrambling up to the top of the first boulder, then leaping to the next.

We reached the top of the ledge and found a narrow plateau. Another cliff face darkened the horizon. Blue tapped his nose against my hip as Robert led us along the flat plain.

Lightning sizzled in my vision, and the sound of thunder mixed with the thropping of a helicopter.

I heard machine gun fire behind us. "That's the calvary," Robert said, his voice tight as we ran.

We reached the cliff face, and Robert began to scramble up the rocks, Blue moving with him. I followed, the intense exercise burning my muscles and shooting sharp pain through my side.

Flagging, my breath coming in harsh pants, I pushed myself on.

There was no time to stop. No time to rest. We had to keep moving if we wanted to survive. We had to keep moving if I wanted to find the prophet.

Robert paused for a moment and looked back at me, his eyes narrowing. Then, he glanced up and pointed. "A cave. We can hide in there."

I nodded, saving my breath. We moved into the cave, it was pitch black and Robert pulled a penlight off his belt, lighting it.

The bright beam cast over the walls, the undulating stone shaking something inside of me.

We all have our purpose, a voice reverberated in my head. *Her* voice.

I grabbed onto Robert's arm to steady myself. My vision flickered, and I grit my teeth, desperate to regain control. But it was like trying to hold onto a snake, slippery and strong, my mind twisting away from me. Suddenly I found myself in two places. I was in this cave but also in another.

I was two people. I was me, and I was Her.

CHAPTER FOURTEEN
EVERYBODY HAS A VOICE

April

Red blotches broke out on his cheeks, throat, and chest.

His shirt was unbuttoned so that I could see the hair growing there, sprinkled with gray now. He dyed the hair on his head black, but his body betrayed his age.

"April, you can't do this."

"I'm already doing it. This is what God wants."

He stood up, his fists balled. We were in the lobby of the Omni Hotel in mid-town Manhattan, so he couldn't go too crazy. He couldn't hit me or scream at me. Not if he wanted to maintain his reputation. "April, I will not let you use my position to spread these lies."

I looked up at him, as cool as a cucumber, my heart rate just as steady as it was before he joined me here.

Before I laid out the facts for him.

"Bill, sit down. You're acting hysterical." I glanced over at Cynthia. She had her phone out and was recording us. His eyes followed mine, and when he saw it, his face grew even redder, but he sat down. "You're recording this." His voice came out as a hiss.

It was the snake that gave the apple to Eve.

"Of course I am. I'm determined. I'm not sure why you're fighting me."

"Because you will be spreading lies," he ground out.

"Lies? So you don't believe that she is a prophet from God?"

"Of course not. That's absurd." He sat back in the chair, crossing his legs and shaking his head. Bill knew what he knew. And he knew that I was a fool.

But he was wrong. Wrong about so much.

"You will introduce me tonight, and I'm going to give a sermon. And the people in that arena are going to love it. They're going to hear the word of God. Because God will speak through me."

Bill barked a laugh. "God will speak through you?" He leaned forward and licked his lips, his dark brown eyes bearing into me. "You're a loser. Without me, you're nothing."

A smile pulled at my mouth. "Do you know what I found? While downloading the photograph of my passport and driver's license from our Cloud account?" I'd lost all my paperwork and was totally destitute when I met Cynthia and the other women on their mission. But Bill always kept our important documents in the cloud for easy access...just in case of an emergency.

"You found nothing," he said, but I could see his mind racing around inside that skull of his, trying to figure out exactly what he'd left in that Cloud.

"You were so smart to keep all our paperwork online," I said as I pulled out my new phone. Cynthia had bought it for me. She and her friends had paid for everything that I wore.

Of course, as soon as I'd gotten back into the states, I'd headed to the bank and repaid them with the nice, big wad of cash I'd taken from the ATM. Bill hadn't bothered removing me from our accounts. He underestimated me so greatly that he was making this almost easy. *God was on my side.*

"Bill." I clucked my tongue against the roof of my mouth. "I can't believe you left this for me to find. But then again, God wants me to be able to control you. To use you for this mission."

I unlocked the phone and navigated to the photos. He and his secretary taking selfies…wouldn't be damaging if either of them were clothed.

You couldn't see that they didn't have pants on, but it could be assumed by the fact that they didn't have shirts on, her pert young breasts and their tight pink nipples pressed together for his inspection as he held the camera out and took the shot.

"You let the devil in Bill, and now God has come to correct it."

He flipped through the photos, his face growing redder. "This is blackmail. You're as horrible as your daughter. As sinful."

"This is what God wants. He wants this message spread. We decide our own value, Bill."

I took the phone back from him and stood up. "I'll be backstage. See you soon."

It wasn't until I was waiting for the elevator back to my room that my heart started hammering. Cynthia stepped up next to me.

"He'll introduce me." I nodded, feeling the truth in my bones.

"Do you know what you're going to say yet?"

"I'll let God speak through me. The message will be spread." I nodded again, the words soothing my rapidly racing heart. "I had to manipulate him. It was vital."

"God wouldn't have given you those photos if He didn't want you to have them. If He didn't want you to do this."

I looked over at Cynthia. She'd become a close friend and confidant in the last two weeks. Had gone with me to the consulate to get my new passport, had flown back on the same flight as me. Our rooms were next to each other at this hotel. Her friends had all needed to return to Florida at the end of their mission, but Cynthia had no obligations.

She was a widow, and her children were grown. She had nothing more important to do with her life than help me. God had brought us together, and together we would change the world by spreading Her message.

EK

I pushed my palms together, feeling sweat between them. Bill paced the stage, his voice booming over the crowd. *He would announce me at any moment.*

I'd been on the stage with him hundreds of times, but never given a sermon. I'd always said something simple and brief, something about the importance of donating, the importance of letting God into your life.

But I'd never brought forth the word before.

I felt it welling inside me though; it pressed at the inside of my skull. My limbs tingled with anticipation, and I stepped from one foot to the other, trying to release some of the nervous energy.

Cynthia stood next to me, her eyes riveted on Bill.

"I've got about five minutes," I said, needing to fill the silence.

"Have some water." Cynthia offered me an uncapped plastic bottle.

I took a sip, and had trouble swallowing. Nerves were choking me. *What if my voice abandoned me?* That couldn't happen! I steeled myself against the thought.

Cynthia took the bottle back and nodded. "You're going to do great. *He* is with you."

I nodded again. "Yes. I know."

And then Bill was introducing me. "Now, as I mentioned, I have a very special guest. Many of you know her already—my wonderful, beautiful, faithful, amazing wife, April Madden." People applauded. "She's just returned from a mission to the Middle East." The crowd grew quiet. I squinted against the stage lights, trying to make out faces in the audience, but I couldn't see them. "While in Syria, she met a prophet."

Bill's voice went quiet, solemn; it was his 'this is very important, lean closer so you can hear me better' voice.

He was doing it perfectly. I knew he would. Bill was a showman. And he wasn't going to let the show be ruined just because he was being blackmailed.

"Now, I want you all to listen to her. You don't have to necessarily believe her."

A murmur ran through the crowd. What did that mean? Why would he say such a thing?

"God is in your hearts, and he will tell you what is truth. But she needs to testify to all of you."

Bill moved out from behind his pulpit, striding across the stage, casual and sleek. For a big man he moved lithely—as if the spirit helped carry some of his weight.

"April has been a woman of God for many years now. He lifted her out of alcoholism." Bill's voice rose. And a murmur of assent went through the crowd with a few *amens* rising up. "He carried her through the loss of her son and daughter."

Sympathetic noises now; many in the crowd knew my story. How Jesus had saved me from so much sin and misery.

My heart squeezed. Had Jesus saved me? Or had the devil led me into that pit of pain? I shook my head. I needed to keep it clear, keep it open for the Lord to speak through me.

"So you know she has Jesus in her heart." More amens. "And you know she's a woman of God." The crowd grew louder; they liked that kind of thing. *A woman of God.*

"So please, listen to what she has to say. And make up your own minds. Let God help you decide."

Bill turned toward me, and I stepped out onto the stage, my low heels clicking on the wood, the lights hitting me in the eyes. I forced myself not to squint into the glare. A smile spread across my face as I approached Bill.

I belonged here.

Bill reached out, taking my elbow, and leaning down, he brushed a kiss against my cheek. His skin was slick with sweat.

"Thank you," I whispered against his ear. He stepped back and held my gaze, cocking his head slightly—as if he was seeing me for the first time. Maybe he was. Maybe it was the first time I'd ever revealed myself to him.

I stepped up to the pulpit as Bill left the stage.

I must reveal myself to this crowd, strip away all pretenses, and let the truth shine through me.

"Good evening." My voice boomed back at me, and I pressed on. "I traveled to the Middle East, looking for my daughter."

The crowd shifted toward me, liking the story. They always like a narrative.

"I loved her very much. But I had forsaken her." I took the microphone from its stand and walked out from behind the pulpit. Pacing helped the words move through me.

"We hadn't spoken in years. But a mutual friend called and told me my daughter was in trouble. So I went looking for her."

More murmurs. *They understood; of course you went looking for your child.*

"I thought that she had fallen in with the devil."

More murmurs. The crowd felt my fear...they had experienced the same thing themselves. "I thought that because we didn't see eye to eye, she was a sinner." I stopped pacing and turned to the crowd, growing very still. "And I was right, she was a sinner..." A beat of silence. "But so was I."

Some amens rang out in the quiet hall. "I was a sinner for many years. The devil whispered to me, and I listened. With the help of Bill and the strength provided by Jesus, I was able to ignore his call to drink, to booze it up, and hide from the pain inside of me." My voice rose, taking on some of that swing and swagger that Bill had. The crowd moved with me—beginning to dance to my beat.

"So," I began to walk again, looking down at my feet, gathering my thoughts. "So I went looking for my daughter, to save her." I turned to the crowd, staring into those bright lights again, letting them catch my irises so that they'd glimmer for the crowd. "And what I found... what I found was true salvation."

An excited murmur. *They all craved true salvation.*

"See, my daughter was a sinner. But she was saved. Saved by a prophet."

Whispers traveled through the crowd. No one talked about modern-day prophets. No one believed in prophets anymore. As if God couldn't reach us now so directly, in this world of sin.

"I didn't go looking for a prophet; I didn't go looking for a renewal of my faith. But I found it. This prophet. She saved my daughter. She brought her back from death!" The words poured out of me, effortless and true. I stepped forward, to the edge of the stage, and raised one hand to the sky, my palm opened toward the crowd.

"And I have witnessed. I have witnessed miracles. And I have seen the work of God." The crowd leaned forward. I had them enthralled.

No, it wasn't me.

It was God.

"This prophet is a woman." Voices in the crowd reached me. *What did she say? Impossible. Liar.*

"A woman who covers herself from head to toe to remind us that we are all one. That we are all *Her*. Men and women. We decide our value." I pushed against their doubt. "It is not up to the people around us; it is not up to society. It's up to each individual to know their worth. To know that inside them is God. To know that we are all his children. That we are all equal."

An uncomfortable edge filled the room. Everybody equal? That's not how this worked. There were sinners, and they were saved. There was white, and there was black. There were men, and there were women. There were Christians, and there were Muslims.

There was God, and there were humans.

"I sense you don't understand me. Or you don't want to understand me. And I get it. God has been saying this since the beginning of time. But we have been ignoring him. We have misunderstood him for human history. Our own egos, our own need to place something above another, has led to this time we live in. The sins of man have ruined our planet, have caused war and strife. And chief among those sins, ladies and gentleman, is our refusal to acknowledge our value."

"Now." I stepped back, my voice dropping. "I know this is hard to believe. But let me tell you what I saw. Let me tell you everything..."

The crowd leaned closer. *I had them.* The word was reaching them.

Anita

I gripped my phone, staring down at the screen. Messages continued to ping.

"Anita, what's wrong?" Tom asked, his hand at my waist, warming me through my thin T-shirt.

I stepped away from him, sucking in my bottom lip and grinding it under my teeth.

"Anita, talk to me, please." I tore my eyes off the screen and forced myself to look at him. His hair was tousled, his lips plump, his cheeks reddened.

"I need a minute." I stepped further away from him.

Tom reached out, but I quickly left the small kitchen. "I just need a minute," I said again, running to the bedroom.

I closed the door and sat on the bed, scrolling through my phone.

There was mention of the Miracle Woman, and the prophet and her "war against men," as some far-right groups were calling it. But Joyful Justice and the name Sydney Rye had not appeared yet.

That could only be a matter of time. Someone was going to realize the connection—they'd figure out that Sydney Rye aka Joy Humbolt was the Miracle Woman in the video.

We had to disavow her. Joyful Justice couldn't become the army of the prophet. It wasn't what we'd set out to do. It wasn't our role. Joyful Justice helped anyone who needed us. Not just women. And not because God told us to. No matter how much the message aligned with ours we could not borrow the prophet's voice.

The men's rights activists were having a field day. Saying that this Miracle Woman's bloody rampage was evidence that the Her Prophet was violent, that the goal was to kill men and upend the social order, not to bring equal rights to women.

It would only get worse from here. This was going to hurt a lot of women.

I texted Dan, telling him that I was monitoring the situation, but at this point I thought we should just stay quiet.

The video would be cut up and turned into propaganda for Isis, for white supremacists, for chauvinist groups of all kinds...a violent woman was a powerful drug to these groups. She proved the necessity of their own violence, their insistence on oppression.

A knock at the door stilled my fingers over the small keyboard of my smart phone. "Anita, you okay?"

I needed to get him out of here.

Standing up, I crossed the room and opened the door. His eyes flicked to the bed behind me, sending a hot blush sweeping over my body.

"Are you okay?" he asked.

"Yes, something work-related has come up. I need to be alone."

"But, Anita. Can I help? Is there anything I can do?" He raised his eyebrows. He looked so sweet, and kind...and safe.

I wanted safety. I hadn't let anyone touch me since the attack, and Tom's had felt right. *Maybe...*

"I just..." My phone pinged again, the sound making us both look down at the screen. I tilted it away from his gaze.

"What are you up to, Anita?" asked Tom, cocking his head, a glint coming into his eye—he was too smart, I'd never be able to hide my association with Joyful Justice from Tom. *He had to go.*

"Nothing." My voice came out edged with anger. Who was he to question me, anyway? We were no longer a couple. We weren't even friends.

I pushed past him and headed for the front door.

"Anita, please. I'm sorry. I'm sorry. I just...I don't want to lose you again, not when I just found you."

I kept walking, steeling myself against his words. Steeling myself against the urge to turn around and kiss him, to let him take away my worries for the night. To let him support and hold me.

"I just can't, Tom."

"Why not?" Tom demanded. We were in the hallway now. I took his coat off the rack and held it out to him. "Please, Anita, I'm begging."

I shook the coat, trying to get him to take it, but he refused.

"Tom, I need to work."

He dropped to his knees, his hands pressed together in the position of prayer.

"The only way you can conquer me is through Love, and there I am gladly conquered." He quoted Krishna from the *Bhavagad Vita*. He'd given me a beautiful copy as a wedding gift. Tom knew how much the text meant to me. He knew those words would spear me right in the heart.

Tears burned my eyes, and my nostrils flared as I struggled to keep them inside me. He just stayed there on his knees, waiting for me to answer, not pushing, not leaving...just being.

I couldn't get him involved. It would ruin his life.

"Tom, you can't be with me. It's..." I dropped my hand, letting his coat go. It landed on the floor in a pile "It's impossible."

"Nothing is impossible."

I shouldn't tell him, but I wanted to...

More of the *Bhavagad Vita* came back to me. *The Gita is not a book of commandments but a book of choices.*

"I'm a member of Joyful Justice."

"What?" His expression hardened.

"That's right, Tom. That's why we can't be together. You can't be with a fugitive. You can't be with someone who's under investigation by Interpol."

"Interpol knows about you?" His eyes narrowed—the lawyer in him coming out. "Then you need an attorney."

"They don't have my name, but they could at any moment—they know I exist." I shook my head. *Why hadn't he left yet?*

Tom stood up and stepped closer to me. "Anita," he whispered. "Let me..." He placed his left hand on my hip, and I stiffened, trying to fight the comfort that it brought me. He pulled me flush against his body, and I didn't push him away. I didn't have the strength. "Let me stay," he whispered, his lips brushing my forehead.

"The mind is restless, turbulent, obstinate and very strong, O Kṛṣṇa, and to subdue it, I think, is more difficult than controlling the wind."

Tom's touch stilled the storm inside of me. I tilted my head and pressed my lips to his, releasing myself into the quiet of him.

CHAPTER FIFTEEN
CLOSING IN

April

Cynthia, her eyes welling with tears, embraced me as I stepped off the stage. "You were brilliant!" she yelled over the cheering crowd. Bill was already back out there, encouraging them to donate.

He was a master, and I needed to learn from him.

Bill closed out the show, reminding his flock to sow their seeds and invest in God. "Put money in the collection plate so that it can come back to you tenfold!"

He left the stage to crashing waves of applause. Sweat darkened his hair and shirt. When Bill passed me on his way to his dressing room, his scent washed over me—I'd loved that smell once, but now he reeked of greed to me.

I stayed standing on the side of the stage and watched the house lights come on, watched the crowd gather themselves, and felt the energy drain from the space as they flowed out the doors.

Cynthia tugged on my sleeve. "We should go. There is still work to be done. I've got the footage." We'd recorded my testimony, and we needed to go back to the hotel and work on creating a reel for me. If I wanted to spread the word, I needed to get on TV. To do that, I needed something to show producers.

I ran my arm through Cynthia's, and we navigated through the bowels of Madison Square Garden and out onto the sidewalk. The streets were packed with people. Clouds hung low above us, glowing with the lights of the city. The buildings and bustling people seemed to soak up the light and energy of the night sky, taking on its brilliance and majesty, leaving the heavens dulled.

The crowd from the show still lingered. They walked arm in arm, carrying swag bags and chatting excitedly. A couple spotted me and ran over. "You were amazing," gushed the woman, grabbing my hands. She looked to be in her early thirties, with owl-like glasses and mousy brown hair,

I squeezed back. "Thank you."

Her husband stood behind her, holding a tote bag with Bill's logo on it. "Can I get a picture please?" she asked.

I nodded, surprised but pleased. A ripple of vanity passed through me...*How was my hair?* It didn't matter, I sternly reminded myself.

We smiled as her husband snapped a photo with his phone and then they moved on. Cynthia squeezed my arm. "You got through to them," she said. "You're gonna change the world."

"And you shall help," I told her.

A man in a dark suit, a foot taller than me and wearing sunglasses even in the dark of night, appeared in front of us, startling us into a stop.

"April Madden. Please come with me." He gestured to the street where a black SUV with tinted windows idled.

My heart rate spiked. Cynthia pressed closer to me. "You're not taking her anywhere," Cynthia said, her voice wavering.

"Please, ma'am, step into the vehicle. Both of you," Sunglasses said.

Another man climbed out of the SUV and stood behind us, his cold, dark eyes shadowed under the brim of a baseball cap with HSI embroidered on it.

"Who are you?" I asked, my voice firm, my faith straightening my spine.

These men could not hurt me.

"Homeland Security, ma'am. Please get in the car."

"I'd like to see some ID." I unlinked my arm from Cynthia's and balled my fists at my side.

Sunglasses reached out and grabbed my arm. I tried to step back, but Ball Cap was there, and I bumped against him.

Within seconds they'd dragged me over to the car. I tried to twist free, but it was like trying to break away from a vise. The back door opened, and I was pushed inside, Cynthia bundled in after me.

Sunglasses got in next, and Ball Cap came around. When he opened the door I tried to climb out, but he pushed me back in.

The four of us were squeezed into the back seat of the SUV, Cynthia and I practically in each other's laps. We merged into traffic and inched along toward Times Square.

"What do you want?" I asked, opening my purse. "I'm going to call 911. This is kidnapping."

Sunglasses took my purse and pulled it free; he didn't even have to yank.

"Ma'am, please remain calm. You are in no danger."

"That sounds like a boldfaced lie to me," Cynthia said, splotches of red brightening her cheeks.

"We're investigators from Homeland Security, ma'am. We need to ask you some questions."

"About what?" I demanded.

"About your recent trip to the Middle East, ma'am."

I clenched my jaw and sat back against the seat, wiggling my shoulders until I fit, determined to not be afraid. *To be brave and have faith.* The car moved through traffic, headed downtown. We eventually pulled up in front of a high-rise in the Financial District.

The men climbed out, and Cynthia and I followed. Sunglasses took my arm, and Ball Cap kept a firm grip on Cynthia as they moved us through an empty lobby.

They used keycards to call the elevator and then we descended. The doors opened onto a cement hallway that looked like it could survive a bomb blast. They moved us down the hall and into a bare room with two metal chairs and a table between them. An interrogation room.

"I'd like a glass of water, please," I said, my throat dry and muscles tense.

Sunglasses nodded and left us alone with Ball Cap.

Sunglasses returned a moment later with a cup of water for me. "Cynthia McDaniels. I'll take you with me now."

Cynthia's eyes found mine, and I gave her a small nod.

No man could hurt us. We were soldiers of God.

Cynthia and Sunglasses left, leaving me alone with Ball Cap.

"You know my name, but I don't know yours," I said.

He didn't even crack a smile, just remained standing by the door. I sat down in one of the chairs and put my water onto the table.

Twenty minutes passed—I prayed, giving thanks to the Lord for the powerful evening, and assuring him that I had faith that whatever was happening was all a part of his plan. That I was prepared to pass any test.

When the door finally did open, I was jerked out of my reverie and blinked a few times as the man entered and came into focus. He looked somewhat familiar, but I couldn't recall from where.

He was handsome, with dark hair and eyes, tanned skin, and broad shoulders that tapered to a narrow waist. He wore a dress shirt and suit pants but no jacket. His sleeves were rolled up, exposing strong wrists and a gold watch.

He smiled and took the seat across from me, laying a folder on the white tabletop.

"Mrs. Madden. My name is Declan Doyle. I have a few questions I'd like to ask you."

"What kinds of questions?" I said, my voice scratchy from my sermon earlier.

"Your daughter, Joy Humbolt aka Sydney Rye, a known member of Joyful Justice."

I straightened my spine, reaching out and taking a sip of water. There wasn't a question there, so I didn't bother answering him.

"When was the last time you saw your daughter?"

I counted the days in my head. "About two weeks ago."

Declan Doyle smiled, his eyes brightening. "Is that so?"

He opened the folder and pulled out a photograph, placing it in front of me. I leaned forward to look. There I was, wearing long robes and crouched over the body of Nadia, on the stage where she'd died. A shiver ran over my body. *God needed to take her.* It was the right thing. I mourned her loss but did not grieve for her.

He threw another picture on top of it. My daughter, on that same stage, staring into the camera.

"You saw her at the battle of Surama," Doyle said.

"That's right." I nodded.

"Do you know where she is now?"

I shook my head. "But I know what she's doing."

"Really, what's that?"

"God's work."

He barked a laugh.

"Ma'am." He sat forward so quickly that I flinched. "Your daughter is one of the most wanted fugitives on the planet." His eyes glittered, and my heart began to beat rapidly. "And you're not going anywhere until you tell me where she is..." He held up a finger. "What she's up to..." Another finger. "And how I can find her." A third finger popped up.

Suddenly I felt the weight of all the earth on top of us. I felt the pressure of the walls around me.

I was a prisoner.

FK

Anita

I met Angela at a bar in SoHo. It was all dark wood, candlelight, and martini glasses. She sat on a high stool, her tailored suit crisp even after a long work day.

The Friday happy hour crowd jostled and swayed—people yelled over each other, gesturing with their drinks. I maneuvered through the crowd, each body pressing against me, sending shivers of fear over my skin. I breathed in the scent of the place—stale beer and spilled gin—reminding myself that I was in London. No one was seeking to hurt me. I was safe.

Spotting me, Angela waved, her platinum watch glinting in the low light. She gave me a big smile and slipped off her stool to embrace me.

Her perfume overpowered the other smells in the bar and I closed my eyes, taking her in. We hadn't seen each other in three years, not since I walked out on Tom and left the city. But we'd stayed in email contact.

I'd lied to her.

The way I'd lied to everyone in my life. She thought I was still a journalist, living in New York, working mostly as a freelance editor...that explained why my byline never showed up anywhere.

"How are you?" She yelled over the rumbling at the bar.

I nodded and smiled, "Good, good. You?"

She bobbed her head side to side in an impression of me. She loved that Indian mannerism. An Irish girl whose skin was so white it was practically translucent, we'd met in college. She'd studied communications while I studied journalism so we'd had some classes together.

She'd even taken me home to her family one Christmas. Their thick accents and even thicker sweaters warmed my memories. Her father, drunk and singing, his arm around his daughter, smiling at her. Angela had one of those families that hugged and laughed and loved all loud and out there.

Angela waved down the bartender and raised an eyebrow at me. "What are you drinking?"

I ordered a glass of Cabernet and Angela gestured to her glass, asking for another.

"It's a Manhattan, in honor of your place of residence." She lifted it up to me before taking the last sip.

We slid onto our bar stools, and she asked again how I was doing. Again, I told her good.

"You're working at Finnigan, Inc. now," I said.

She nodded taking another sip of her drink. "Yeah, the hours are hell, but the pay is amazing. Never would think the daughter of a sheep farmer could afford this, did you?" She held out her wrist where the platinum Rolex sparkled.

I smiled. "That's great. I'm really happy for you. Anyone special in your life?" I asked.

She did her head bob again, a small smile creeping onto her lips. "I've been seeing someone." She shrugged. "Nothing special. What about you? Tom called, you know. I told him where you were." She turned as our drinks arrived. I insisted on paying and then fiddled with the stem of the glass.

"Yes, Tom showed up at my place last night." My cheeks heated, and I hoped the dark bar would hide my blush.

"Did he? You know he's still madly in love with you. Poor man. I can't ever imagine why you left him in the first place. Rich, gorgeous, successful. What more do you want, Anita?" she said in a teasing tone of voice, but the question was really there.

"I wanted to stand on my own two feet," I said boldly. She held my gaze.

"And you couldn't do it standing next to him?"

I shook my head. "No. I couldn't."

She nodded, thinking it over and then turned back to her drink. I took a sip of my wine, and we sat in silence for a moment.

"Well, I guess I get that. Maybe that's why I haven't met anyone special yet." She looked over at me. "But you know, Anita, it's not like he's trying to take your power." She paused, staring into her glass for a moment. "I think we women—" She gave me a sad smile. "We give it too easily. Our power, we just hand it over like it's nothing, not realizing it's not easy to get it back."

I nodded. *She understood.* And her understanding unclenched something in my chest.

"So..." Her voice had turned teasing. "You saw him last night? How did that go? You two always did have some pretty intense energy." She cackled at herself.

My cheeks heated even further. "It's complicated."

She leaned forward waggling her eyebrows. "Oh really, tell me more."

She'd always been like this, teasing and fun. Taking nothing particularly seriously. She was a breath of fresh air to me. And I felt, with a sudden pang, how much I had missed her. How much I had missed these easy female friendships.

I'd hidden myself away ever since the attack. Hadn't let anyone touch me. But more than that, I hadn't let anyone joke with me, play with me. I'd been so damn serious. And I thought that was somehow regaining myself. But the fact was that *this* was regaining myself. This easy drink in this crowded bar with an old friend.

"So," I said, changing the subject. "Seen any of our other old friends around? I tried to get hold of Rida, but her number's no longer working."

Angela's face fell and her gaze turned serious. "Oh, God, you haven't heard?"

"Heard what?"

"She went back to Syria, right before Isis." She turned away, her eyes shimmering. "I haven't heard from her. I'm afraid...I think she's probably gone." Her voice was barely a whisper.

"Oh, no," I said. "When was the last time you saw her?"

"Right before she left. She'd been on the phone with her mother, begging her family to come to London. She'd offered to pay. Everything. But they were being stubborn. The civil war had largely spared their village, and the threat from Isis had yet to materialize. Rida was devastated, frantic. As I'm sure you can imagine." Angela took a sip of her drink. "She told me she was going to get them." She shook her head, tears welling in her eyes and catching her words, distorting them.

"Isis moved very quickly," I said.

"Yeah, quicker than Rida could have imagined. She flew back there with plans of dragging her sisters onto the plane, if nothing else, but within days after she left here her village was surrounded. And there was no way out." Angela looked up at me. "She called me." Angela swallowed, and swiped at her eyes. "The last time I spoke to her she said... she planned to kill herself rather than be taken prisoner."

I sucked in a breath. "No."

"I hate to think of that, but better than..." She left the sentence hanging, the horror of becoming a prisoner of Isis thickening the air between us. A shudder ran over me as I pictured my brave, brilliant friend at the mercy of those heartless zealots.

"That's terrible. Horrible," I said. We sat in silence for a moment, the gaiety of the bar around us almost insulting to the memory of our friend's struggle. "Rida never was religious, at least when I knew her. Do you think that changed?"

Angela shook her head. "You knew her. She wasn't a practicing Muslim. I mean, you know she had all that stuff in her head. The way we all do." Angela waved her hand in the air. "I mean, I was raised a Catholic. The guilt is overwhelming." She gave a small laugh. "But no, she never went in for that kind of stuff. It's half the reason she left Syria."

"She just never fit in there," I said, remembering our long talks about the countries we were from, and how they didn't fit us. How they felt like corsets, sucking our breath away.

"Exactly, she was so brilliant though." Angela took the final sip of her drink and then shook the ice in it. "You know," Angela said, looking up at me. "She was one of the best surgeons in the city, and so many fine surgeons," she raised her brow, "*men* in that profession, come to think of themselves as gods. But Rida was never like that. She always remained humble. Always stayed grounded." Angela looked back to her drink. "I miss her."

I bit my tongue. *She may not be gone.*

EK

As I walked down the hall of the apartment building, my mind ran over my conversation with Angela. How could Rida change so radically? Is that what loss did to people? Could it change *everything*? Our very purpose?

I put my key into the lock of the apartment door, and it creaked open without turning the key. My heart rate spiked, and I stepped back, the blood rushing in my ears as I tried to listen for any sound of someone inside.

I know I locked it.

Scrambling in my purse, I pulled out my mace and my cell phone, the best weapons a woman in London can have.

I toed the door open, my mouth dry and heart hammering.

Light from the hallway threw an eerie yellow glow into the darkened apartment, casting long, sinister shadows. From the entrance, I could see into the kitchen, where light from a street lamp spilled in through the window. Pots and pans littered the floor, the cabinets all stood open, and the paper towel roll lay unfurled across the counter.

The place had been ransacked.

Should I go in? Or call 999?

I had no right to the general police services. I couldn't involve them. Couldn't risk them finding out about me.

Should I call Dan?

I listened hard, hearing only the traffic from the street below and the low whisper of a neighbor's television. Holding my breath, I stepped into the darkened apartment and flicked on the hall light.

The bathroom door to my left stood open, the shower curtain ripped down, exposing an empty tub.

Raising my mace, I continued down the hall and turned quickly into the living room. Light from the street lamp shone through the big windows and bathed the place in its anemic yellow glow. Feathers coated the room, the couch cushions splayed on the floor, cut open. I flicked on a light, bringing it all into stark reality.

My eyes grappled with the situation. And my heart beat even faster as I realized that my laptop was gone.

Shit, shit, shit.

I moved forward through the living room, toward the bedroom. The door stood ajar. The mace still tight in my grip, my finger on the trigger, I pushed open the door and flicked on the light.

The closet doors were open, the contents spilled everywhere. My suitcase was ripped to shreds, as though someone had cut into it with a knife looking for secret compartments. They'd taken my laptop, but at least I still had my phone, cash and ID—which I'd kept in my purse with me.

I backtracked through the apartment and went into the kitchen. Pouring myself a glass of water, I gulped it down, my heart still racing.

The laptop was encrypted. Dan took these kinds of things very seriously. It was unlikely someone could break into it...but with time?

I dialed Dan's number and he picked up immediately.

"Dan, the apartment has been ransacked. My laptop is gone."

A beat of silence. "They won't be able to get into it. It has a self-destruct mechanism."

"I know, but..." *What?* "Who would do this? What the hell is going on?"

"Get the hell out of there. Get the hell out of the country. Go. Now. I'll arrange a plane for you out of London City Airport." His voice came out strained, harsh.

I didn't need to know who did this or why. I just needed to get the hell out of there.

I wasn't a part of the investigative arm of Joyful Justice. *I wasn't supposed to be here.* I was supposed to be safe, helping control things from behind the shadows. One of the wizards behind the curtain.

I put the glass down on the counter, my hand shaking.

"Okay, I'm going."

I disconnected and turned toward the door, clutching at my purse. I stepped back out into the hallway, and closed the door. I turned the key in the lock, but the thing was broken. Adrenaline made my fingers shake. *I had to go.*

My phone pinged and I glanced down at it. Everything stopped moving. My eyes zeroed in on the screen.

"April Madden Gives Rousing Sermon at Madison Square Garden—Claims to be Mother of the Miracle Woman."

I unlocked the screen and a video popped up: Sydney Rye's mother in front of a massive audience.

"Holy shit," I whispered.

I had to go right now. I could look at all of this on the way to the airport.

I turned and slammed into a hard body. A man's arms wrapped around me, and I screamed.

HER PROPHET

Do you think your story will be told? Have you done enough to warrant this moment? To explain *your* existence? That is what we are all fighting for. The answer to *why am I here?*

CHAPTER SIXTEEN
TEMPEST

Sydney

The sound of distant gunfire reverberated through my mind, punctuating the rolling thunder that crashed over me, wave after wave. Candlelight flickered in my vision. Water dripped onto stone. The iron-y tang of blood and the sharp pain of my injuries overwhelmed my senses.

My lips were moving. I was speaking.

We decide our own value. God has sent me to tell you this.

A woman's face came into focus above me. Brown, intelligent eyes and hollow cheeks. Her skin was almost the same color as the sandy stone of the ceiling. The candlelight flickered off of it in the same undulating waves. *She saved my life.*

Lightning crossed my vision, and my Savior disappeared behind it.

"Sydney! Sydney!"

Robert's voice broke through the storm. His fingers, digging into my biceps, ripped me from the memory—or was it a hallucination?

Blue's nose pushing into my hand anchored me to reality.

I blinked, and Robert's face came into focus, his green-blue eyes glinting in the low light of the cave. The only illumination came from the beam of his flashlight, which now lay on the cave floor, lighting one wall, as if waiting for dancers to enter the stage.

"Sydney," Robert said again, his voice lower. He could tell I was back. "Sydney, where did you go? What happened?"

I didn't answer him. I didn't know. Was it possible the voice I'd heard inside my head, the one I thought was the prophet...was actually my own?

No. I wasn't the prophet. I was the Miracle Woman. *I was the lie, not the liar.*

"Sydney." Robert's voice dropped low, serious. "You are ill. I need to get you to a doctor."

I shook my head, breathing in the desert air. It was cold and dry, and the deep breaths helped to clarify my vision, helped to chase away the lightning.

But what had I seen? *I had to go on.*

"I need to find out," I said.

If it was possible that the prophet was somehow my creation, I had to know. I couldn't just go back to Miami or wherever it was that Robert wanted to take me. I couldn't just let him take care of me.

Not yet.

My knees buckled, and I fell against Robert. He held me tight to his chest. His lips brushed my forehead as he pleaded with me. His voice faded, and I drifted away. Drifted to that other cave. To that other place. To that other woman.

The voice you hear is not my own. I am a messenger from the Lord. I have come here. Come back from the dead in order to bring equality to this world.

My Savior nodded as she replaced the bandages on my side. I felt no pain, only a kind of floating—like I was high on pain killers. I dragged in a breath, my lungs rattling, and smelled the musky scent of dogs.

Blue pressed his nose to my cheek, and I turned to look at him. He licked my nose, and I laughed, the sound strange—ill—mirthless. My eyes focused beyond Blue and saw a white dog, gigantic and beautiful. Perhaps an albino of some kind. I'd never seen anything like it.

More bodies moved, and I sensed that there were dogs everywhere. There was a pack around me, sent here to protect me.

"They are here to protect me. For I am the voice of God. But also his hand. And you." I turned back to my savior; she paused in her ministrations and found my gaze, blinking, as she waited for me to continue. "You will be my voice. You will be my shield. I will transform the world, and you will be my instrument."

Blue's whimpering made me turn my head. But he wasn't whimpering—he was just lying on the ground curled up with the white dog, the cave around them glowing and flickering with firelight. His whimpering reached me again. And then the sound of gunshots. I turned back to the woman, and she flickered in the candlelight, her face changing from my serene, placid savior to Robert Maxim's furrowed brow and bright eyes.

I blinked, and shook my head.

I sucked in a breath, smelling at once the dogs and the cave and the desert night and Robert Maxim, but also the acrid scent of gunpowder and the musky scent of sweat.

The floating sensation left me, and I could hear Robert. "Sydney, Sydney come back."

"I'm here," I told him.

"I'm getting you out of here. I'm getting us straight back to the States. You can't argue with me anymore. I will not continue this madness."

I almost laughed.

He didn't know how mad it was. He didn't know how deeply, deeply mad it was.

I didn't argue with him, though. I had my answer.

The woman who had saved me, the surgeon who had performed a miracle by saving my life, was guiltless.

My hallucinations, the drugs she must've had me on, made me lose it and come to believe I was an instrument of God.

I had set out to stop her. Only to discover that I was Her.

Robert

EMILY KIMELMAN

I held her close and she trembled against my body. *So vulnerable*. The scent of her wafted over me; sand, sweat, blood, and grit.

"Sydney, are you okay?"

She nodded against my chest. "Yes, just..."

"Just what?" My voice came out harsh, I wanted answers.

She steadied herself and pulled back from me. Her eyes found mine in the darkness. She assessed me for a moment. "I promise you, I'm all right." *Liar*. "Let's move deeper into the cave."

I schooled my frustration. *She was right*. Once the US operatives had dealt with the Isis fighters, they would search for us. We needed to stay hidden. We might even be able to find another way out.

I held my flashlight, illuminating a path, and Sydney stepped carefully as we navigated deeper into the cave.

It grew narrower, and the ceiling lowered. A tunnel split off, and I aimed my light down it. The sound of water dripping and the fresh scent of an underground stream wafted on a soft breeze. Blue whined and began toward the sound.

Sydney and I followed Blue, having to drop to our hands and knees to crawl through the narrow passage after him. It opened up suddenly into a large cavernous space.

I grazed the light around us and saw stalactites in the ceiling far above—their strange shape alien under the torch's bright beam. A stream passed through the cavern, slipping over smooth rock. Blue trotted down to the water's edge. "We could probably follow this out," Sydney said.

I grunted in agreement. "But we should rest first—it's safe here."

Sydney nodded before heading to the stream. She knelt by the water's edge and washed her hands and face before cupping a handful to her lips.

"You can rest," I said, dropping my pack to the stone floor. "I'll keep first watch."

We need to wait at least eight hours before returning to the outside world. Even then we needed to be careful. They wouldn't give up looking for us. While I didn't fear for my own safety, if Sydney fell back into Martha's hands, I might not be able to help her.

My influence with Martha, while strong, was not limitless. Martha wasn't easy to control. I had no dirt on her. She was in no way vulnerable to me. No husband or children. A sister who'd passed away several years ago. No close friends.

She was the perfect counterintelligence operative.

She would make an incredible asset. I'd offered her work before, and she'd turned me down. I'd have to offer her more money...or perhaps power is what she wanted.

Sydney and Blue curled up on the ground, their backs pressed together. I washed in the stream, the freezing water making me gasp. When I turned off the flashlight, pitch blackness enveloped us.

The night ebbed away, the soft, slippery swish of water running over rock and the occasional sound of Blue or Sydney shifting in their sleep the only sounds. My watch, its face lit up in toxic green, told me that dawn had broken, but no light reached into the cave.

When Sydney woke, she said my name. "Yes?" I answered, my voice coming out rough.

"Where are you?"

"I'm right here." *I'll always be here for you.* I turned on the flashlight, illuminating a path through the darkness—though the shadows around us stayed true black.

Sydney came to sit by me, pulling her knees up and resting her chin on them.

"You go ahead and lie down, get some sleep," she said.

"I'm fine."

She looked over at me, those gray eyes searching my face. *What did she see?* "Okay, let's follow the water, then, and see if we can find a way out."

We ate protein bars from my supplies and then followed the stream. The water sparkled in the flashlight's beam as it ran over smooth, sand-colored rock.

Blue walked next to Sydney, his nose rhythmically tapping her hip.

"What will you do when you find her?" I asked, my voice echoing in the chamber.

"I'll talk to her. I'll ask her what happened after she rescued me," Sydney answered quietly, not looking over at me.

"So you no longer plan to kill her?" *What changed?*

"I'm not sure." She stopped and turned to me, her eyes meeting mine. *I couldn't read her.*

"Did you remember something?" I asked her.

"No." Her answer came too fast. *She was lying.*

"You can tell me, Sydney. I want to help you."

Her laugh echoed in the giant chamber. "No one can help me Robert. No one."

EK

Sydney

Our footsteps echoed in the cavernous space, the sound of water running over smooth rock a welcome constant.

I followed Robert's flashlight beam, carefully placing my feet so as not to slip. My senses were on high alert, my body tingling with fear and my mind uncomfortable with the new realization.

It was my voice I was hearing.

Not some woman claiming to be a prophet from God, *but my own voice.*

Thunder rumbled in my mind, and Blue's head twitched toward the sound. I heard the thunder again, and Robert stopped walking. "You hear that?" he asked me.

"Hear what?" I asked, confused. Did he mean the stream? Did he mean our footsteps? Could he mean the thunder in my mind?

"Sounds like a storm."

A giggle escaped me, and Robert turned, the flashlight landing on the water and sparkling there. "What?" His eyes narrowed. "You okay?"

I stifled a laugh. "I hear thunder," I said...*all the time.*

"This could be to our advantage. If there's a storm, it'll make us harder to track. Give us a better chance to escape." Robert started walking again. "It's also a good sign that we can hear it. Must mean there's an exit coming up."

We walked on in silence until the flashlight beam landed onto the entrance of a dark tunnel leading off the cavern. Thunder rolled again, and Blue's ears perked toward that passageway.

"That must be the way out," Robert said, headed toward it.

When we stepped into the space, the temperature dropped, and a shiver ran over my skin. Soon, a glow appeared at the end of the tunnel, and wind whispered along to us. It carried the scents of thunderstorm and sand with it.

"It might be a haboob. It's the season," Robert said.

"A haboob?" I asked, quirking a brow, managing to find the word funny even in this dire situation.

"Yes, it's when a thunderstorm picks up sand and basically creates a wind, rain, and sand storm. They're pretty normal around here."

"Yeah, this region's just full of awesome stuff."

The glow of light grew larger, and we soon stepped out into what looked like mid-morning. To the south, a storm front of massive and gurgling, dark clouds above a sand-colored explosion blotted out the sky and horizon. I'd never seen anything like it. It was moving toward us, the wind picking up my hair and playing with it.

"I think we should wait in the cave till it's done," Robert said.

I looked north, the direction that Robert had said the prophet's cave was.

"The guys looking for us, they'll probably give up during the storm right?"

"Probably," Robert said. "It's not like they can fly in it."

I looked at his profile; he was staring at the storm. The lines around his eyes deepened as he squinted at the approaching clouds. Silver and black stubble coated his jaw and neck, giving him a roguish air—like he was a pirate or a marauder.

"You know, back in 2015," Robert said, "a storm similar to this one but stranger...narrower...hit the border between Israel and Syria, creating a wall that kept a surprise Isis incursion out of Israel long enough for the Israelis to mount a defense. People said God did it. That God protected Israel from Isis."

"Oh, yeah, you think God's doing this, to protect us now?" I asked him.

He shook his head. "No. But I think that people will take anything and make it mean something. If that meaning makes them right. If it helps them to reinforce their ideas." He looked over at me, his green blue gaze sharp.

"What are you saying?"

"Just what I said. No other meaning."

"Do you think I'm making up a meaning? About you?"

"I think you believe that I'm your enemy. That I can't be trusted. Because if I could—" He stepped closer to me, his hand reaching out and taking my elbow lightly. "Because if I could be trusted, if you could lean on me, then so much of what you've believed would be wrong."

There was no right and wrong, only here and now.

"I want to keep moving." I gestured my chin in the general direction where the prophet should be. "I think we can make it before the storm."

Robert raised his brows, and a small smile twitched onto his lips. "You think we can move faster than that storm? At minimum, it's moving at 20 miles per hour. Could be up to 60." He raised his gaze to the storm again, narrowing his eyes. "It's dangerous. It can suffocate you."

"Are you afraid, Robert Maxim?" There was teasing in my voice, and he looked back at me, smiling, his eyes glittering in the morning light.

"I'll do as you ask. But please remember that I did. That I have faith in you."

I swallowed, uncomfortable with his words, with the lack of guile in his gaze. *Could he be sincere?* No, Robert Maxim probably had an ulterior motive. He always did.

EK

Robert

We moved north because she wanted to. The storm clouds chased us, the sound of the sand in the wind screeching through the valley, the threat of death howling all around us.

Sydney led with Blue by her side, their steps in sync, the path apparently known to them. Had she remembered something? Or was this a habit, something subconscious—she'd walked it so many times that she didn't need to *know* how to go, she just went.

The small, pebbled sand crunched under our boots. *We couldn't make it.* But we wouldn't die. That storm would surround us, beat us up, suck us dry, but we'd come out the other side.

That was my faith: in myself.

As the wind caught us and the first sting of sand cut at my jaw, I sealed my lips and followed closely.

A crack of lightning and the landscape jumped into sharp relief—giant boulders, steep passages, a terrain perfect for hiding in. A terrain difficult to navigate in the best of conditions.

Another low howl joined the winds, and Blue stopped walking, straightened his neck, and called back, the sound eerie and powerful. In the distance a bark came in return: deep and gruff and mournful.

Blue whined and looked up at Sydney. She reached out a hand and touched his shoulder before flicking her wrists. He left her side like a bullet exploding from the barrel of a gun, streaking up the hill and disappearing behind a boulder.

The storm engulfed us; the sand blasted my exposed skin and tore at my clothing. The wind screamed in my ears. I reached out blindly and caught Sydney's hand. She twined her fingers with mine, and we leaned into the wind, walking uphill, eyes closed against the assault, the earth beneath our feet and Sydney's touch my only guiding posts.

Sand clogged my nose, and I coughed, sucking in more grit. Sydney stopped, and I bumped against her. She stepped back into me. We'd reached a cliff...I could just make out an edge beyond her feet.

Where did that come from?

A hand gripped my elbow, and my head whipped around, shocked by the human presence so close. My eyelashes battled the sand as I took in a black, cloaked figure—a woman in a full burka stood behind me, her hand tight on my arm.

She pulled on me, and I followed her lead, Sydney's hand still in mine.

The stranger ran her gloved hand down my forearm and grasped my hand. I could feel the warmth of her through the thin material.

This must be *Her*. The powerful, enigmatic figure who'd convinced—how many now? A million?—that she spoke for God, and that her message was one of equality for women.

Was she mad? Or brilliant? Really, she must be both.

Thunder rumbled through the air, and another crack of lightning lit up the storm around us—all ochre and burnished gold. The landscape had lost all definition, replaced with this whirl of color.

The prophet led on, her step steady and knowing. Suddenly, a cave mouth yawned in front of us. We passed through its archway, and the storm was at our backs. My skin burned, the thrashing of the storm lingering in a million small abrasions. The wind echoed in my ears as the prophet lead us deeper into the cave. Sydney's hand stayed wrapped in mine—it felt fused to me, like we could never be apart again.

I looked back at her. Her skin was roughened and red, her hair a tangled, confused mess. Sand filled every crease of her clothing, piled in the crook of her collarbones, and clung to her lashes. She blinked, dislocating grains of sand that tumbled down her cheeks.

A presence at my knee drew my attention—a giant mastiff, golden as the sand, larger even than Blue, walked next to me. *It helped shepherd us here.* The dog's black muzzle was stained the same ochre as Sydney and me.

The prophet squeezed my hand, and I looked forward. She stopped and turned to me. Through the mesh of her burka I could see a glint of eye—the shimmer of a living thing under all that cloth. "Welcome," she said, her voice deep for a woman, her accent English.

I blinked and took in the cave around us. About 40 feet deep and 20 wide, with a curved ceiling and a rock cropping covered in fur blankets. A darkened fire pit sat at its center. Large golden mastiffs lay on the bare ground, their heads up and ears perked, watching me. A bright white mastiff sat in the far corner, Blue by her side, puppies squirming around her.

"Joy, how are you?" the prophet asked Sydney.

"Joy?" I said, turning to the masked woman. "She told you her name was Joy?"

She nodded. "Yes. Joy Humbolt. I'm Rida Dweck. And you are?"

I turned to look at Sydney. She'd gone pale, her eyes wide, mouth parted in surprise. Blue bounded over to her and leaned against her leg.

"Joy is dead," she said, her voice low.

The prophet shook her head. "No, I saved her, and in return, you saved me."

"But..." Sydney stopped speaking, her eyes going hazy with thought.

My God. Her mind had split. Sydney Rye and Joy Humbolt—the hardened warrior and the frightened, vengeful girl—now lived simultaneously inside that one body. She was switching back and forth between her current and former self.

How did I miss it?

CHAPTER SEVENTEEN
SLIPPING THROUGH

April

I pulled in a slow deep breath and felt calm wash over me. "I want a lawyer," I said.

Declan's expression didn't change. That *I know more than you* smile stayed on his face. But one dark brow inched higher.

"Do you? Why's that?"

"I want a lawyer," I said again.

He sat back, wincing slightly. Did he have some sort of injury?

"April." He used my first name, trying to get me to feel comfortable with him. So masculine, to one moment threaten and the next coddle. He was hoping to trick me into revealing something. To somehow incriminate myself.

"Am I under arrest?"

He shook his head slowly.

"In that case I'd like to leave."

"I can't let you do that."

"You can't just keep me here. It's against the law." My voice sounded stern and steady but my heart was beating as fast as hummingbird's wings.

"Ma'am, this is a case of national security."

We were back to ma'am.

"I'm no threat to national security. I'm a mother, a wife, and a preacher."

The left side of his mouth curled up just slightly, and his eyebrows both rose this time. "Yes, a preacher. I just watched your sermon. Interesting stuff."

"Are you a believer, Mr. Declan?"

He shook his head slowly.

"Well, neither was my daughter."

"Is she now? A woman of God?" His voice peaked with curiosity. And there was something more than professional interest there. I cocked my head staring at him. Where had I seen him?

"I know you," I said.

He nodded slowly. "You might recognize me. I was the lead investigator on Joy Humbolt's case. After she killed the mayor of New York."

I tried to keep the surprise off my face, but I could see that he saw it. "So you have it out for her," I said.

"I'm interested in justice. I'm interested in the truth."

"The truth is *His* word. There is no other truth."

"Let's talk about your daughter. How did she seem when you saw her in Syria?"

He had evidence that I'd been there with her. But I still didn't want to answer him. Didn't know if I'd broken any laws of man. Didn't want to get locked up now. I had too much work to do. On Thursday, Bill and I were meeting with radio producers. *I had a message to spread.*

"What do you need from me to let me out of here?" I asked.

Sometimes you must make a deal with the devil in order to serve the Lord.

"Just your full cooperation. Tell me everything that happened. And you can walk out of here."

"Really? I'd like to speak to a lawyer about that. Get something in writing."

Declan nodded slowly. "All right, do you have a lawyer in mind?"

The only lawyer I knew was Bill's attorney. We used him for all sorts of things, but nothing criminal. Would he be able to help me here? If not, he'd probably be able to recommend someone at least.

A knock on the door interrupted us. Declan looked up as it opened and a woman entered. She wore a black suit and a curly clear wire came out of her ear, clearly some sort of communication device. "Sir."

Declan stood up. "I'll be right back," he said, his voice tinged with annoyance. He didn't like being interrupted.

The door clicked shut behind him, and I waited in the brightly lit interrogation room.

I would tell him the truth. I would get a lawyer to help me make sure that none of it could incriminate me and then I would tell the truth. It would be good to have it on record, so that when mankind looked back at this moment, they could hear my story. So that it would be in the official records of the US government.

Filled with a sense of purpose, I waited patiently. Doyle returned moments later, his brow deeply furrowed and eyes stormy.

"You're free to go," he said.

"I am?"

"Yes." His answer was curt, a knife slicing through butter.

I stood, unsure. What was this? Were they going to track me or something? It didn't matter if they did. They were welcome to watch. They were welcome to see me change the world.

I was escorted back upstairs by Sunglasses. Cynthia was already waiting in the SUV.

We greeted each other quietly, but neither of us spoke, both realizing that something strange had happened. Why had they let us go?

They returned us to the street corner where they'd picked us up, without a word. Cynthia and I, back on the street, surrounded again by those crowds and bright lights of the city, turned to each other.

"What happened?" I asked Cynthia. "Did they ask you questions?"

"Yes, they were asking me all about you. How we met. And then, all of a sudden, they let me go."

"Something very similar happened to me. Except that my interrogator, Declan Doyle, had photos of me and Joy in Syria. Taken at that awful place—" I choked on the memories of Nadia's death: the scent of dust and debris from that moment, the blood pulsing from her wound, warm and gushing against the cloth I pressed into it. Anguish rippled through me.

Cynthia squeezed my hand, seeing my hurt, and I pulled in a deep breath, finding comfort in her touch and in the faith Nadia and I had shared.

"Why did they let us go?" Cynthia asked.

"I don't know. I had agreed to answer their questions, to tell them the entire story. I just wanted to talk to an attorney first."

"Of course," Cynthia said. "We have nothing to hide."

"But why did they let us go?"

"It must have been God's doing," Cynthia said, nodding to herself.

But while I could see God's hand in all of this, there was something else. There was another hand in motion here.

EK

Anita

"Hey, hey, hey—slow down."

It was Tom. Adrenaline thrummed through my system, my heart hammered, and my throat was raw from the scream that I had released.

But as I looked up at him, at his concerned expression, his beautiful eyes, the small smile on his lips, I felt suddenly, inexplicably safe. His arms around me didn't feel like they were imprisoning me, they felt like they were supporting me.

Tears welled in my eyes, and I shook my head. *I had to leave him, again.*

"What is it, what's going on?" he asked, his brows furrowed and his gaze concerned.

"I have to go. I have to go *right now.*"

The brief moment of respite I felt in his arms evaporated. The apartment had been ransacked. Whether it was one of Joyful Justices' enemies, a law enforcement agency, or something else entirely, I didn't know.

"What are you talking about? We just..."

"My place, it was..." Instead of explaining further, I pushed the door open. Tom looked past me into the space. His mouth formed a small O of surprise.

The ding of the elevator pushed me forward. I needed to go. I tried to brush past Tom, but he turned and followed as I headed for the stairs.

"Anita Brown?" a deep voice asked from down the hall. I turned toward the elevators; two men in overcoats approached us.

Tom straightened next to me, and I despised myself as I moved behind him. *Hiding behind a man.*

"Can I help you?" Tom asked, taking control of the situation immediately.

The man in front, wearing a gray fedora and a sour expression, stared past him to me.

"Anita Brown. We'd like to speak with you."

The other man, shorter and broader, was bare-headed, and his curly dark hair was cropped short.

"Who's asking?" Tom asked Fedora.

The man reached into his overcoat and pulled out an ID. Flipping it open, I saw the badge of an MI5 operative. *Oh, shit.*

"MI5," Tom said, his voice even, as though he wasn't worried. "Well, it's lucky her attorney happens to be here."

Tom reached into his own overcoat pocket and pulled out his wallet. He withdrew one of his cards from inside the fine leather. He passed it to the man.

Fedora's brows rose. "You two were married, right? Mr. Brown." He looked up at Tom, a smirk pulling at his lips. "She left you."

I glanced up at Tom, who returned the man's smirk with one of his own. "Yes, I see you've done your research. But that doesn't mean I can't represent her."

"We'd like to speak to her."

"I'm standing right here," I snapped, stepping next to Tom. *Talking about me like I wasn't even in the room.*

Tom turned to me, and his eyes glittered. He was asking me to let him handle this. It was his domain. He was the barrister.

"We just have a few questions, ma'am, if you'll come with us."

Tom put his arm out, blocking me, and Fedora caught his gaze.

"Is she under arrest?"

"No," Fedora almost growled. "But we have some matters of national security we'd like to discuss with her. I think she'd want to help."

"She'd be happy to help. At a time of her convenience. You can call my office to set up a meeting. We have dinner reservations."

Fedora settled back on his heels. His partner, Curly, stepped forward.

"You think you need an attorney?" he asked me.

I didn't answer.

"Have you done something that you would need legal representation for?" He cocked his head, all innocent curiosity.

I pressed my lips together, refusing to answer.

"Like I said." Tom smiled. "Call my office to set a date. Now, if you'll excuse us?"

He took my elbow and began to lead me toward the elevator.

"You forgot to lock your door," Fedora said, as I passed him. We were so close that his breath brushed my hair. "That's dangerous in a city like this." I looked up at him. "You never know who's wandering around."

"You don't need to worry about her," Tom said, pulling me down the hall. "We've got everything under control."

As we waited for the elevator, the two men watched us. Tom checked his watch, looking completely casual—as though he was concerned about a dinner reservation.

He was playing it so cool, and I was shaking with fear.

I shouldn't have come here. I wasn't part of the investigative arm of Joyful Justice. I belonged behind the curtain. But something in me didn't want to stay hidden anymore. I didn't just want to manipulate from afar, I wanted to get in and fight.

Tom looked over at me and smiled, his eyes sparkling as the elevator opened. We stepped in and turned toward the closing doors. Fedora and Curly still stood in the hall, watching us. As the doors closed, Fedora tipped his hat to me.

Tom put his arm around me and pulled me close to him.

"What's going on? Please, Anita. Let me help you." I shook my head. "I can't lose you again." There was a beat of silence. "I'll come with you."

My head jerked up, and I looked at him. "You can't. You can't give up your life for me."

I'd never give up my life for him.

"I can," Tom said, his voice deep and rough. "And I will." He took my hand and led me off the elevator and out onto the street. A mist made the street lamps look like crystal balls. Tom hailed a taxi, and I blindly got in with him.

"Where to?" he asked me.

"London City Airport," I said.

The taxi merged into traffic. Tom's fingers stayed entwined with mine.

Could I let him come with me? Could I have faith in this? Could we be together?

I wanted all of those answers to be yes.

EK

Tom looked like he belonged in the luxurious cabin of the private plane. He was typing on his iPhone, sending an email to his firm, telling them he was taking an emergency leave of absence.

He'd called his mother from the airport and explained that he'd be in contact again soon—that he was taking a much-needed vacation.

The way he was just giving up his life, just dropping all the things he had worked for, astounded me.

Then again, I'd done the same thing when I left him. Years of establishing myself as a reporter, establishing myself as his wife, and I'd walked away from all of it because I wanted something else. I wanted freedom, and the knowledge that I could stand on my own.

And now Tom was giving up everything because he wanted *me*.

It felt too good, to be loved like that. I'd always known that he enjoyed spending time with me, that I could make him laugh, but I'd always felt stifled by his position, by his social status.

And now he was taking himself out of that world for me.

Rida came into my mind again. She may still be alive. Or perhaps she

had been murdered or taken her own life, and whoever had saved
Sydney Rye was someone else entirely.

But I didn't think so. Rida had changed. Maybe she'd lost her mind
and thought she was hearing the voice of God. Or maybe she'd gotten so
sick of the abuse, of that constant oppression that all women of color
feel, that she'd decided to do something crazy.

She understood the power of faith. The power of religion. It's what
kept her parents in Syria even as Isis came for them.

It's what drove Isis.

And now it was driving women all over the world to, for the first
time in their lives, recognize their value.

I scrolled through my own phone messages. April Madden's Madison
Square Garden appearance had gone viral. Even as some people were
celebrating her message, she was being attacked as anti-male and anti-
Christian.

She had a lot more enemies than followers, if the comments on the
YouTube clips were to be believed.

But the fact that she was getting this traction, that this message was
spreading, whether it was people's outrage over it, or faith in it, didn't
matter. The Internet didn't care if something was good or bad, only if it
connected.

What about Joyful Justice's message? We'd always been very careful
to have a simple message.

We fight for justice.

If you need help, you can come to Joyful Justice, and we will train
you and help you defeat your enemies. But, as the Internet raged with
the Her Prophet's message, as God's name was thrown around,
appearing to be on everybody's side, where did Joyful Justice stand?

April claimed to be the mother of the Miracle Woman. That her
daughter, Joy Humbolt, wasn't dead, but alive and wreaking havoc in Isis
territory. People were starting to believe her.

She'd had a following as the wife of an evangelical preacher. And now
she was creating one of her own.

Something sparked in my mind. A realization that I shied away from
at first.

Joyful Justice needed a manifesto. We needed an outline of our plans, a clear set of rules for everyone to follow.

And I was the one to write it.

I looked over at Tom again, and his eyes flicked up to me. He smiled.

A shiver ran over my body.

Did he understand what he'd gotten himself into? Was there any possibility he could know?

Maybe he didn't care. Clearly he had faith in me. *In us.*

That faith gave me strength. I felt it welling up inside me. This was the strength of connection. This was the strength of community, partnership.

I felt it with Joyful Justice, and yet I stayed hidden. I'd hidden behind Twitter handles and Facebook accounts, because I didn't want to be imprisoned. I didn't want to be on the run. I didn't want to be a fugitive.

But that time had passed. It was time for me to come out. It was time for me to step from behind the curtain.

"Do you have any paper with you?" I asked Tom.

He smiled and cocked his head. "Sure," he said, reaching into his briefcase and pulling out a yellow legal pad and a pen. He passed it to me.

"What are you working on?"

"I have an idea..." My old instincts crowded in, telling me not to share with him. Telling me to keep it close to my breast until it was perfect. Until I'd constructed the perfect argument. But I gathered my strength to push past that instinct, and I said, "I'm writing a manifesto. Will you help?"

He stared at me for a moment, his expression unchanged, and then a grin spread across his face.

"I'd love to."

CHAPTER EIGHTEEN
THE DEVIL'S PATH

April

Bill's laugh traveled through the telephone, sending tingles of fear down my spine. "You've got nothing on me anymore. If you expose me, I'll expose you right back as a blackmailer." His words bit into me. *He was right.*

"I did it to spread the message," I said, my voice soft. *I sounded beaten.*

"No one wants to work with you. And they'll want to work with you even less if they find out that you're a blackmailer." Each word spread like venom through my veins, poisoning me.

I stood up from the bed and paced away until the phone cord tugged me back.

"I am going to speak at your next big gathering," I said, keeping my voice calm, trying to sound strong.

He laughed again. "You're not. And no one is going to give you a radio or TV show."

"My sermon is getting more views than any of yours ever have. Someone will help me spread this message. If it's not you, it'll be others. We will not be silenced." I sat down on the bed, feeling a great weight on my shoulders.

"The sermon might be getting a lot of views, but so is the video of you in Syria. Holding an AK-47. Jesus, April. I didn't even recognize you. You're not a woman of God anymore. You're working with the devil." His voice dripped with disgust.

"I am not." I shot to my feet. "You wouldn't know the voice of God if it was screaming in your ear!"

"I am a man of God. And I have sinned and I have repented." His voice began to take on that lulling, sing-songy quality he had when talking about his faith. That tone that had brought him so many followers.

I'd watched the video of my sermon at Madison Square Garden. I had passion and a good story, but couldn't match his showmanship.

But the comments on my video didn't care about that...death threats had been pouring in. I'd had to get a new phone number because an anonymous handle on Twitter released the number and the calls had been non-stop.

You'll die bitch.

I'll fuck you before I kill you.

You deserve to be raped and murdered.

"April, now listen to me," Bill said, talking to me like I was a child. Like I didn't know my own mind. Like I didn't know God's will. "I'm willing to take you back. Let's go to the ranch. We'll figure out what to do about this together, how to get you out of this mess."

My heart hammered in my chest. There was a part of me that wanted to do that. To fall into his arms.

Wives, submit yourselves to your husbands, as unto the Lord.- Ephesians 5:22

You decide your own value.

"No, Bill, I'm not done yet."

"I won't be able to help you soon, April. If you don't repent, you'll be lost. 'Women should remain silent in the churches. They are not allowed to speak, but must be in submission, as the law says.' First Corinthians 14:34"

I slammed down the phone, anger coursing through me.

Then I heard that whisper, that slithering voice in my head, telling me...*just one little drink.*

My eyes locked onto the mini-bar. I knew what was in there. Little bottles filled with liquor. Vodka would smell so good. Taste so good. Give me just a little rest.

You deserve it; you've been working so hard. It's a good idea to take a break. That's when solutions come.

I walked over to the fridge and opened it up. Just to take a look.

Bill was wrong. I could do this. I had to have faith.

I slammed the fridge closed and paced away from it. But I was drawn back to it like magnet to metal. Like waves to the beach.

The cracking sound of the little cap coming off sent ripples of pleasure through me. I'd just give it a sniff. *Not drink it.* Just one little sniff.

The Gray Goose smelled like an old friend, like home. It was as if I had been on a long journey and walked back into my kitchen. It wrapped me in the comfort of familiarity.

My lips parted, and the plastic rim touched my tongue as I took *just one little sip.*

Just enough to ease the tension. And help me think.

But one turned into another. And then another. And soon I moved on to the brown, to the bourbon and the rye. Then I was in his arms, the devil wrapped around me, his tongue down my throat and his voice controlling my mind.

EK

Stinging cold hit my face, and I gasped, sucking in water, sputtering and coughing. Lunging upward.

A strong hand held me down. They were drowning me!

"You stay in that water." Her voice was harsh, not to be trifled with.

I turned my face away, gasping for air, escaping the freezing water. It soaked my clothing, and I shook with the cold.

"April!" A hand slapped my face so that my gaze suddenly faced upward.

Cynthia hovered above me, her shirt splattered with water, her brows knit together. I stared up at her as the freezing water poured down over my head, and my teeth chattered. We were in the bathroom at the hotel. What happened?

My mouth felt coated in grime. I swallowed, tasting liquor. I groaned, my head throbbing. Cynthia reached up and turned off the hand shower.

Tears, hot against my freezing face, dripped down my cheeks. A giant sob racked me. *I failed.* I couldn't do this—the devil won.

Cynthia stood, and offered her hand to me. I didn't take it. I couldn't get out of the tub. Couldn't do any of it. I shook my head.

"Take my hand," Cynthia demanded.

"No, I can't. The devil has me."

"Only if you let him. Now give me your hand."

I looked up at Cynthia, my vision blurred with tears. Her pudgy cheeks were pink, her mouth a thin line of determination. "I won't let the devil have you," she said, her voice loud in the small bathroom.

"But, how can I? How can I preach if no one will listen?"

"You'll preach the way you were meant to. The way God wants you to." Cynthia reached down and grabbed my bicep, hauling me up. I wavered on unsteady bare legs, icy water dripping off my T-shirt.

Cynthia grabbed a towel off the rack and threw it over my head. She scrubbed at my hair, shaking me so that I almost fell. But she held me up.

I felt like a child under her ministrations. "Now you listen to me," Cynthia said, pulling the towel down to my shoulders and wrapping it around them. "We've got work to do. A message to spread. You're important."

She was looking straight into my eyes—hers were the color of the Caribbean Sea. I wanted to be by that sea. I wanted to sit in a lounge chair with a margarita in my hand and disappear into that beauty.

Cynthia helped me out of the tub and escorted me back into the bedroom. She pulled out clothing, outfits we'd bought together. Skirts and jackets that we felt were modest and yet powerful.

The price tags were high. New York decided the value of these clothes. And people judged your value on what you wore.

How could the prophet's message ever reach enough people without television or radio?

I picked up my phone, and Cynthia grabbed it out of my hand.

"I don't want you looking at your phone anymore." Cynthia said, throwing it onto the side table.

"Why not?" I asked, trying to reach for it. She picked it up and shoved it into her jean pocket.

"Because, the things people are saying about you are nasty. And they're not going to help. They're going to drive you back to the bottle."

She dusted off the jacket she wanted me to wear and threw it onto the bed.

"I'll run downstairs and get a cup of coffee. You get dressed. You have a sermon to give."

"I do? Where?"

"Just because we can't get on TV right now—" Cynthia said, turning to me, her hand on the doorknob. "Doesn't mean you can't preach the word. I reached out to our sisters in Florida, and they reached out to their families here. You've got two churches to speak at tomorrow."

She opened the door and left, taking my phone with her.

My stomach twisted, and I had to lunge into the bathroom to grab the toilet bowl in time. I heaved, bringing up all that was left in my stomach. The disgusting taste of old alcohol and stomach acid filled my mouth.

How could I do this?

FK

My stomach lurched as I entered the church, and the scent of wood polish caught me. If there had been anything left in my stomach, I would have lost it.

But I was empty.

My head throbbed, and my heart hammered as Cynthia and I moved down the aisle, slipping into one of the front pews.

The minister was a friend of a friend of Cynthia's. Young and interested in what I had to say, he'd watched the video of my sermon and was willing to let me speak. He came up to us as the pews filled with worshippers.

"April, Cynthia, wonderful to meet you," he smiled, revealing dimples.

"Thank you for having us, Father." I smiled as he took my hand.

His hazel eyes held mine as we shook. "I look forward to hearing you speak." He excused himself to prepare for the service, and Cynthia and I waited for the show to begin.

This part of Queens was still middle-class people—some of the few surviving real New Yorkers. While Manhattan became overrun by the super-rich and Brooklyn by all those godless young people with tattoos and piercings, out here a normal family could still scrape by.

In a way it reminded me of the town I'd grown up in—Beacon, New York. An industrial city in the last century, Beacon had been left to die on the shores of the Hudson River along with the fish and other animals poisoned by the chemicals from the manufacturing boom.

But here, in the midst of a thriving metropolis, they still had work.

The people that filled the pews around us were dressed in their Sunday best: cheap fabrics and ill-fitting clothing. But they were clean, and pious, and ready to listen.

A buzzing filled my ears as the minister took to his pulpit. I couldn't hear a word until Cynthia nudged me.

"And so I'll ask you to listen to her. And, as Bill said, make your own choice."

He gestured for me to come to the stage, and I stood, my head spinning from the hangover and the lack of food. But as I made my way up to the pulpit my stomach settled, and the throbbing behind my eyes dulled. I faced the crowd and took a moment to survey them.

Unlike the stage in Madison Square Garden, I could see their faces. I could see the children squirming, the men dozing, and the women looking haggard and tired—all of them staring at me, waiting for me to speak.

"I never would have believed in a modern-day prophet if I hadn't seen it with my own eyes," I said.

My voice echoed through the nave, confusing me. The sound system wasn't set up properly. Like the parishioners' clothing, it was ill-fitting and cheap.

But, I forged on.

"Can we all not agree that we must decide our own value?" People shifted in their seats, but nobody nodded. Nobody agreed.

I faltered, the congregation watching me, their eyes narrowing. They didn't want to hear this. I wasn't making sense. I stepped away from the microphone, the echo too much for my throbbing head.

"Can you all hear me in the back?" I called, projecting my voice.

I saw a few nods.

"I want to tell you my story. And I thank you for listening."

I told them how my own belief that I knew better than God had lost me my children. "Because I thought to judge as God judged, I turned my children away."

A few heads nodded. Mostly women. A few men's faces turned sterner. Judging was a pastime, a reason to come to church. It made you better than your neighbors.

I went on, telling the same story I told to Cynthia and her friends, the same story I told in Madison Square Garden. When I was done, I returned to the microphone. A bible sat open on the pulpit, and I touched it, running my fingers over the smooth, thin paper.

"Thank you," I said, my voice echoing back to me. "Thank you for listening."

I sat down next to Cynthia; she smiled and nodded at me. I hadn't whipped the crowd into a frenzy the way that I'd done in Madison Square Garden.

Yet it was the same story. So what was different here?

When the service ended I stood and made my way toward the exit with Cynthia. A woman stopped me, a child asleep on her chest, a toddler holding onto her hand.

"You really think we decide our own value?" She asked me.

"I do," I said.

Her eyes ran up and down my suit, taking in the expensive clothing.

"You've obviously got money." She said it like an accusation, as though somehow that made me evil, made me wrong.

And that's when it occurred to me. This wasn't like Bill's church.

These people came here to stay out of hell. They came here for protection. People came to Bill's church for heaven. They wanted to sow the seed that would bring them wealth. Sow the seed that would bring them salvation.

That's who I needed to reach. People who wanted what I had—not people who were just trying to keep their heads above water, too busy treading to think about stroking.

"Yes, I've been very lucky in life. God has taken care of me."

She sneered. "You think God did that?"

"If not Him, then who?" I asked.

"I don't know, tell me how you bought that fancy clothing, and I'll tell you if it was God or the devil."

My mouth dropped open in shock. "The devil? Why would you say that?"

She stepped closer to me, her eyes narrowing. "I see you, April Madden. I smell liquor on you. And I see the devil in your words."

Before I could respond, she turned and walked away, her child stumbling after her.

"Ignore her," Cynthia said. "There will always be people who don't believe. This is God testing you. Come on, we have another church to get to."

She hustled me out to the rental car. And as we began to drive I finally found my voice.

"What if she's right? What if the devil is speaking through me, not God?"

"That's just not the case." Cynthia said. "Lots of people are going to say horrible things to you, April. But I think you're stronger than them. And I think you're here for a reason."

Her eyes flicked to her rear-view mirror, and I turned to look over my shoulder. A black SUV was following us.

"Oh, my God. Do you think that's...?"

"Yes, they've been following us since this morning." She looked over at me before returning her gaze to the streets. "You're going to have to be strong. Very strong."

CHAPTER NINETEEN
THE PROPHET

Robert

She pulled off the burka, the disappearing stream of fabric revealing her dark hair tumbling in silky waves around her face, large brown eyes lit with fierce intelligence, high cheekbones, a narrow nose, full lips, and a fresh scar on her chin.

The Prophet.

"Please." She gestured toward a rock outcropping covered in pelts. "Sit. I'll get a fire going. Help yourself to some water." She pointed to a bucket with a ladle next to some horn cups.

My thirst roared to the forefront of my mind, and I crossed to the water, pouring some for Sydney and me. We drank it down in gulps. Cool and refreshing, it washed the sand from my mouth.

Sydney moved away from me, walking to the back of the cave to sit by Blue and his puppies. The white mastiff laid her head on Sydney's knee and sighed peacefully.

Looking down at the giant dog, Sydney stroked its head. A puppy climbed into her lap, half on its mother's face, and whimpered for attention. A smile stole over Sydney's face, and she cuddled the big puppy close.

There were four pups, three of which had blue eyes, and one that shared the mismatched pairing of its father. They had Blue's markings— tan and black at their shoulders, on their muzzle and around their ears. Their snouts were something between their parents, not the elegant length of a collie, or the mushed, wrinkled edifice of a mastiff.

Giant paws hinted at their eventual size. *These would be serious dogs.*

A fire came to life under the prophet's ministrations, and she sat back, her gaze finding mine. "You never told me your name."

"Robert Maxim," I said.

"Please, Robert, sit," she indicated a spot across the fire from her. I took the proffered seat and stared at her for a long moment.

"You're the prophet," I said. A hint of awe entered my voice. *How did she do it?*

She shrugged. "We are all the prophet, Robert. We are all Her. My name is Rida."

I shook my head. *False modesty.* "You're the one who made the video."

She nodded. "Yes, I did that." Her eyes traveled over to where Sydney sat with the dogs. "But it was Joy's idea."

Sydney looked up from the puppies, her face deep in shadow. I couldn't see her eyes. Couldn't tell if she was Joy or Sydney. Did it matter? Only in that Joy wanted me dead, and Sydney trusted me enough to travel through a sandstorm clutching my hand.

I returned my attention to Rida. She brought her gaze to meet mine —strength and calm radiated from her.

"How did you..." I paused, unsure of how to ask the question.

"You want to know my story. The story of Rida?" She gave me a small smile.

"Yes. Your accent is British."

She nodded. "But I am Syrian." She paused and looked down at her hands—long-fingered and elegant, but also strong: a surgeon's hands. "I was born in Syria." She looked back up at me. "And here I will die."

I didn't speak, letting the crackling of the fire fill the silence, hoping that she'd continue, explain herself. She gave me a half-smile and leaned back, resting against a rock, reaching out to pet a mastiff who sat nearby. It scooted closer, resting its head by her knee as she massaged its neck.

"These dogs were my father's. They are kangals, the largest breed in the world. He bred them to help with his goats. Except Janan." She gestured toward the white dog. "He gave her to me as a gift when I returned last year. Her name means 'heart and soul.' My father said that with me back home, our family's heart and soul had been restored.

He refused to understand that I was only there to try to drag them back to England with me." She shook her head. "Now I am the only one left. The only survivor." Her eyes found mine and deep sadness shone from the depths of her gaze. "Can the heart go on without the rest of the body, Robert? Without the limbs, the head?" She raised her eyebrows in question.

"You appear to be very intelligent, a skilled surgeon."

She gave me another one of those half-smiles. "You think maybe I was the brain? Not the heart."

I shrugged. "Maybe you are complete on your own."

She shook her head. "No one is," Rida said softly.

Her words made my chest ache. *For so long I lived just for me.* The image of that boy soldier lying in the sand, at my mercy, came into my mind. *I didn't kill him. I didn't kill Mustafa. I was here, instead of safe—here for Sydney. Something inside me had changed. Pursuing my own interests was no longer enough...*

"What happened to your family?" I asked.

Rida glanced at Sydney again before reaching up and touching the scar on her chin. "We are Shia." She paused, frowned. "Were. We were Shia. But I have not believed—practiced— for some time." A soft smile danced across her full lips before it pulled back down into a frown. "I never told my family I didn't believe. They died thinking I still practiced." She shook her head. "But I did not share their faith in God's protection."

She looked up at me, the fire flickering between us. "And I was right. He didn't protect them. Their bodies are in a ditch with their neighbors...with all the others who believed what they did. My sisters, my brothers, my grandparents, aunts, uncles." She stopped, swallowing, her eyes filming, but she continued to hold my gaze. "They died for what they believed in."

"How did you survive?"

Her nostrils flared and anger kindled in her gaze. "They lined us up. The whole village, in groups of twenty. They lined us up in front of the grave they made us dig. Then they fired. And *they missed me*. I fell back, lay still, covered in the blood and corpses of my family and neighbors. I waited there—" she swallowed, "in that pit of death until night fell and then I climbed out."

She looked down at the dog by her knee. "They'd taken my father's dogs, tied them up. They were starving them." She closed her eyes as a tear escaped and dangled for a moment on her long dark lashes before releasing and falling into the blackness of her dress. "I knew if I was going to survive I had to free them. Take them and the goats, and live out here. But I also knew that I had to..." She looked up at me, her eyes bloodshot with the horror of her memories. "I had to kill the men who..." She faltered briefly before continuing. "Before they shot us, they raped the women." Her face twisted with disgust. "My youngest sister was only thirteen."

"I'm sorry."

She shook her head almost violently. "Do not apologize to me." Her voice came out forceful. "No regret can change what happened."

I nodded, looking down at my boots, unable to meet her gaze—it held so much pain and power it felt almost like looking directly into the sun.

"Isis had left only a few men behind in my village. So, I went to my house, and I got my father's guns. I freed the dogs and I..." Her gaze went hazy, her mouth smiling. "No one was on guard because they thought we were all dead. I killed them while they slept."

She paused for a moment. "I have saved many lives, and lost some too, on the operating table. Blood and exposed tissue are not foreign to me. I know how to turn off the part of me that *cares*. My medical training, the decade I spent learning to save lives, allowed me to take them so easily, so...precisely." She shrugged. "I took my dogs, and I went and gathered our animals, and I set off into the wilds—where I knew no one could find me if I didn't want to be found."

"Why didn't you try to get out? Get back to London?"

Her eyes flicked to me and then over to Sydney. "You are a powerful white man, and you cannot imagine a world where you are so vulnerable. But I had no way to move through Syria, no way to get to an airport. No way to escape except the one I chose."

"Surely your friends in London would have—"

She cut me off. "You should listen to me instead of your own vision, Robert Maxim." Her eyes held mine. "I am telling you the truth, and you are denying it to hold onto your beliefs. That is how you end up in a ditch."

My brows rose, and a smile pulled at my lips. "I'm not the kind of man who ends up in a ditch, Rida."

"Are you the kind that asks men to dig them?"

Sydney spoke from her corner for the first time. "He is the kind making money off the two sides thinking any of it is worth the effort."

She knew me so well.

Rida nodded knowingly. "The eye in the sky? A god amongst men."

"I've never claimed to be divine," I pointed out. "Unlike some people in this cave."

Sydney laughed, and I turned to look at her. *Rida saved her life. I owed her.* "How did you come upon Sydney?" I asked, still looking at Sydney where she sat, the puppy asleep on her chest, Blue leaning against her side, the white mastiff's wide head resting on her lap.

"I heard the battle—the gun fire, the helicopters. I'd been staying in a lean-to nearby, and I decided to check it out. Hoped to scavenge from what was left of the wreckage. When I saw Joy laying bleeding on the ground, with Blue by her side, I knew I needed to help her." Rida stared down at her hands. "I wanted to save a life. I had medical supplies I'd taken from the local clinic when I left my village. Painkillers, sterile instruments, bandages."

"You did an incredible thing."

"Yes," she nodded. "I was always an excellent surgeon."

"How did she convince you to...?"

"Claim to be a prophet from God?" Rida asked, her voice even. "She mumbled in her sleep at first, and then she started to make sense. And her words were nourishment to my soul. That women were equal, that it was *our* responsibility to stand up for ourselves. That without women leading our own movement, claiming our own equality, releasing the power within us, we'd never be free. I believed it all."

I nodded, encouraging her to go on.

"The fact that she said it was God telling her..." Rida smiled. "It's not the first time I've heard a post-surgical patient claim to have a direct link with the big man upstairs." Rida gave a low laugh. "People say crazy stuff on those drugs. But it was the combination, the idea that God would sanction a female revolution. That set something inside me free. I *wanted* it to be true. I wanted to believe. And so I did."

"That simple?"

"The same parts of the brain light up when we feel 'the spirit' as when we gamble—our reward centers. It is a very powerful motivator, much more powerful than intellectual thought. Non-religious people sometimes feel it in nature, or when contemplating revelatory scientific theories...it isn't anything concrete. No amount of *thinking* will get you there. Will light up that part of your brain." She gestured around the cave. "I feel it when I walk in this landscape, its vastness and beauty, the safety it has provided for me...I *feel* gratitude that I am alive and free."

"Are you free?" Sydney asked, her face shadowed.

Rida turned her attention to Sydney. The firelight flickered against Rida's skin so that she almost glowed. "Yes, I am. As are many who believe."

"What do you believe in? I don't understand," Sydney said.

"You don't remember anything from our time together?"

Sydney shook her head, creases of displeasure forming around her mouth. "I thought you were my enemy. That you'd been controlling me...using me. Then I came to realize." Her gaze found me in the dim light. "I realized that the words I'd been hearing in my head were my own. But I didn't understand that...they were Joy. I didn't know that I..."

"That you had slipped back into your earlier self," I said, picking up her thoughts, saying the words that were too hard for her to speak.

Rida smiled gently, her eyes soft. "No, I never controlled you. We worked together. Once you recovered enough to slow down your medication, we talked."

"About how to change the world?" Sydney asked.

"Yes, we agreed that the only way was through God—through the reward centers of the brain." She turned to me. "Have you read the *Bhagavad Gita?*"

"Years ago."

"I read it in med school; a friend gave me a copy. You know that the Hindus don't believe in a single God, as Christians, Jews or Muslims do?"

I nodded. "They believe in 'the God Head.'"

"Right. So anyone can be a prophet—we are all God. We all have that direct connection that prophets claim in other religions." She leaned forward and, using a long metal tool, poked at the fire. "If we can change consciousness, we can change the world." She reached behind her, grabbing another log from a pile. "Women must rise up to be equals, or the world will never find balance." Rida placed the log on the fire and the flames engulfed it.

"The world will never be balanced, not in the way you want," I said. "And even if it were, women can be as evil as men. Everyone is guilty."

She gave me that half-smile of hers. "That's true. Everyone is guilty. Women are guilty of believing the lies. As are men. It hurts everyone. I believed all of that, but it was Joy who convinced me that women insisting on their equality will lead to a better world. And she convinced me to insist that idea came directly from God. We found herders, and I showed them her wounds, told them my story—that I brought her back from death with His help. So the word spread. And the miracle was believed."

"But I never wanted any of this," Sydney said, interrupting.

"You did. And you got it."

"But...I'm no longer Joy."

"You're both," I said, a calm coming over me. I looked to Rida for confirmation. "She must be switching back and forth between Joy and Sydney, like someone with multiple personalities, right?"

She shook her head. "I'm not a therapist."

"Just a surgeon," I said.

"How do we know she's not a messenger from God?" Rida asked me, holding my gaze—challenging me.

"Because there is no such thing."

She shrugged. "You can't prove that, and neither can I. But it doesn't matter. What matters is if people believe."

"I recognize that. Belief is the most powerful drug we have."

"Yes, the biggest reward. If you want to change a habit, you must offer a large enough reward to the brain."

I nodded, knowing the science—habits were merely tracks in our brains that led to rewards—the brain didn't care if the reward killed you, like smoking, or made you fit, like running, as long as the brain got its nicotine, its dopamine, its reward.

Sydney Rye was *my* habit—and she had changed me.

EK

Sydney

I breathed in the scent of the puppy: musk and stone and milk. The young dog slept against me, snoring slightly. Totally trusting. His mother—the giant white mastiff Rida had said was named Janan—warmed me, her head on my lap, her chest against my thigh.

Robert and Rida spoke over the fire, but I had stopped listening—their voices rose and fell like a stream babbling in the distance. The cave wrapped me in comfort, despite the terrifying revelations I'd received here. *Joy was inside me—and she wanted out.*

This cave felt like home.

But it wasn't.

My stomach rumbled as the scent of food reached me. Glancing up, I saw Rida cooking over the flames. The smoke rose up and slipped through an opening in the cave ceiling.

Robert stood, his body unfolding elegantly, and approached me. All of the dogs watched him—recognizing the powerful predator he was.

Robert crouched in front of me and held my gaze. "You okay?"

I let out a soft laugh. "I don't know."

He nodded, frowning. "Let me take you back to Miami. Get you help. We can solve this together."

I shook my head. "There is no helping me. I just destroy things."

"That's not true." His voice was harsh, almost angry. "You may have changed the world, Sydney. You may have flipped the script."

"Joy did that. Not me."

"She couldn't have done it without you. Please," his voice dropped, so that it sounded almost like he was pleading, except that Robert Maxim never begged for anything. *He took what he wanted.*

Tears burned my eyes, and I looked down at the puppy in my arms. "What if she kills me?" I whispered, not wanting to let that possibility loose into the air.

"Joy?"

"Yes."

"Maybe you can learn to live together," Robert said. "Work together. Lean on each other."

I looked up, and his gaze was on me. That icy sea behind his eyes a few degrees warmer…he was showing me something.

Lean on someone? Be with someone?

"What about Mulberry?" I asked.

His gaze shuttered, and he looked down at the mastiff resting her head on my lap.

"I will have him transferred to Miami." Robert looked up at me. "You can heal together."

A spark of hope ignited in my chest. Could we really? Could Mulberry and I be together? If I could let go of my fear, and agree to accept help…

I swallowed the emotion choking me. "Okay."

Robert nodded but didn't smile—his face was that icy mask again. *He wanted me to be with him, but that would never happen.*

Robert went to stand, and I reached out, taking his hand and stopping him. "I'm sorry, Robert." His brows raised in a question. "I'm sorry that you want what you can't have."

A small smile played across his lips, and he looked down at our joined hands. "Never say never, Sydney."

A small laugh escaped me. "You don't give up."

He shook his head, still not looking at me. "We have that in common."

I glanced over at Rida. "What about her?" I asked. "Should we take her with us?"

"She doesn't want to come. I can move us out once the storm passes, but it won't be easy."

I stared at his face for a long moment. Golden sand still clung to his dark hair. His eyes, usually so cold, appeared warmed by the firelight.

Robert was right that we were alike; both willing to do whatever it took to get what we wanted. Both selfish.

The puppy stirred, and I looked down at it. He blinked, opening his eyes—one blue and one brown, just like his father. He yawned, exposing sharp little teeth, and then settled against me again, closing his eyes and falling back to sleep.

"We have a long journey, little fella," I told him. "But don't worry—I'll take care of you."

I'd get better, and I'd take care of all of us.

CHAPTER TWENTY
THE CALL

Anita

Dan flipped through the last of the long yellow pages. When he finished reading the manifesto that I had written, with Tom's help, on the journey back to the island, his eyes came to meet mine. "And you want to say this, on a video? With your face uncovered?"

I nodded. We were up in his office. He sat on the black leather couch, and I paced in front of him.

Dan leaned back and put the yellow pad next to him on the cushion. He looked down at his hands for a moment, absorbed in thought. "I'm not sure. What do you think it does for our mission?" He looked up at me. "To have you so exposed?"

"Look, MI5 was coming to talk to me anyway." I started to pace again. "But that's not even the point, Dan. I don't want to hide anymore." I stopped and turned to him, putting my hands on my hips. "I need to be out there. I need my voice to be heard."

"Can't your voice be heard in a more subtle way? I don't want to risk you." His eyes held mine. *He cared about me.* "Not only are we friends, Anita, but you're vital to the mission of this organization. What happens when you're exposed?"

"Joyful Justice needs a representative who speaks our message aloud. I know we make videos with people who we've trained and have completed missions, but *I* want to lend my voice to this movement. One of the problems with the Internet is the fact that we hide behind our keyboards." Dan flinched a little. Here was a man who knew about hiding behind keyboards.

"There is strength in concealment," Dan countered.

"I understand that, Dan. I really do. But the fact is that I don't want to be hidden. I want my voice to be heard."

"You know how much you're going to be attacked. Look at what's happening to April Madden."

"Shouldn't I be as brave as she is?" Dan frowned. "Besides, I'm not going be running around giving sermons. I'm going to make this one video. I'm going to be a voice for change in this world. A voice for women rising up, for obvious reasons. Not because God tells them to, or because now it's all right with the Lord. But because it's just plain right."

Dan pursed his lips and then nodded. "I'll get Jill to set up the recording equipment for you. But there's something else we need to talk about." He held my gaze again. "Tom." Dan smiled. "You just showed up with him. How do we know we can trust him?"

The question felt like a punch in the stomach after his supportive words. "You don't trust me to decide that?" My voice came out harsh.

"I trust you, Anita. I don't trust him."

"They're the same thing. You should trust me, and whom I choose to trust."

A smile tugged at Dan's lips. "You know that's not in my nature."

"What, you think he's a mole or something?"

Dan shrugged. "I don't have any evidence that he isn't."

"He's in love with me." The words spilled out. Was that a defense? One that Dan would understand?

His eyes narrowed. "I know you two were married."

"And he lied to MI5 for me. And left the country with me. And now is sitting in my room, waiting for me to come back after this meeting."

"So he gave up everything to be with you."

"Yes." The truth still astounded me. And a niggling of worry tickled the back of my mind.

"Anita," Dan sighed. "How can that possibly work? How can he possibly just sit around for months on end waiting for you? Is that what you would want?"

"Don't worry; he'll be an asset to us. He's a brilliant barrister. A specialist in international human rights law. He's been fighting on the side of good for a long time."

"Within the system," Dan pointed out.

"Yes, but he's ready. He helped me write that." I gestured with my chin toward the legal pad. Dan glanced over at it.

"Okay, but I want him kept out of this area. His movements will be restricted. And I'm going to run a serious background check on him." Dan looked up at me. His eyes were hard. He wasn't to be argued with.

I nodded. "I would expect nothing less." Warmth ran through me again. Dan worried about the organization, but I could also see in his eyes that he was worried about me, too.

Dan stood and came over to me. I tilted my head to maintain eye contact. "It's good to have you back, Anita." He opened his arms, and we embraced. I rested my head against his chest.

And I felt him smile against the top of my head.

"What you wrote is really beautiful. I'm proud of you." Tears stung my eyes. *This was where I belonged.* "I just want to say one more thing." I stepped back and Dan kept his hands on my shoulders, maintaining eye contact. "You're about to expose yourself. There's no taking this back. You'll be hiding forever."

I nodded. "Actually Dan, this is the first time in my life I won't be hiding."

April

After our Sunday of preaching in New York we traveled south, stopping at every revival meeting and church that would have me. The black SUV and its occupants—two men who wore suits and watched us through their mirrored sunglasses—followed us the entire time. They did not hide from us nor did they interact. We did not know their purpose and after many hours of discussion had given the matter over to God and no longer discussed them. *Maybe they were my guardian angels, or two demons sent to stop me.* It did not change my path.

If not for their eerie presence the time reminded me of the early days of Bill's ministry, except now I was the preacher and Cynthia my support. *It was impossible to act alone.*

We were eating breakfast in a diner in southern Georgia, headed toward Pensacola where I was to speak at a Christian women's conference, when Cynthia's phone rang.

Her mouth opened in surprise and then spread into a wide grin as she nodded. "Yes, yes...we can do that. Thank you."

She hung up the phone, staring at the screen for a moment.

"Who was that?" I asked.

"That was Nicholas Faber's booking agent. They want you to speak at his next revival meeting."

Nicholas Faber. One of the most successful televangelists on the planet. He had two private jets, a compound in Montana, a mansion in Santa Barbara, and a very popular TV show. Bill looked up to him as one of the most successful in the field. *He spread the message far and wide.*

"I met him once," I said. "With Bill. I can't believe he reached out." Tall, blond and in his early sixties, Nicholas Faber was handsome in a classic kind of way—strong jaw, sparkling blue eyes, the broad shoulders of an athlete, and the slightly rounded belly of a man who lived a good life. His smile came easy and often, his words as slippery and seductive as caramel.

"Well, you've been getting a lot of attention," Cynthia said, smiling. She picked up her coffee and sipped. "We've done a great job with your videos. They've been shared a lot."

She still wasn't letting me look at my phone. So, I had to believe her when she told me these things. *I must have faith.* The fact that Nicholas had called proved that Cynthia was right.

My face heated as I pictured the audience I'd be speaking to...in the few weeks that we'd been on the road, I'd developed my voice and found a connection with the flocks I'd spoken to, but this was huge. This was Madison-Square-Garden huge. "It's amazing. I'm so excited. When, where?"

"He's got a big revival happening two weeks from now in Fort Lauderdale. He also wants you on the show the following day." She was grinning again. "Can you believe it? My friends and I traveled from Fort Lauderdale to save souls in Turkey and found you. Now we are going back there!"

I looked down at my pancakes, and my stomach churned. I was too excited to eat. "Do you think I'm ready?" I asked, not looking at her. Could I handle the pressure? Stay away from the comfort of the bottle?

"Yes, I know you are." Cynthia's voice was firm.

I'd used what I'd learned in Syria, speaking to individual women, sharing my message person-to-person, and that had brought me back to here. Brought me back to a larger platform.

Please let me not fall again.

But that was ego—the wrong prayer.

Please let me spread the message.

I shouldn't care how the word traveled, as long as it reached people. *I want it to be my voice.* That was the devil! I pushed him away and looked up at Cynthia. She watched me closely, her blue eyes sharp.

"You can do this," she assured me. I nodded, but couldn't bring myself to answer her.

Anita

I blinked against the light. "Can you move it down a little bit?" I asked.

Jill touched the lamp and angled it so it wasn't directly in my eyes. "How's that?"

"Good." I ran my hands along my pants, drying the sweat. Tom stood next to the camera, smiling.

"You've got this," he said.

A nervous laugh escaped me.

"Remember, we can do as many takes as you want," Jill said.

"Yeah, I know."

Jill's assistant held the poster boards I'd written my notes out on.

Tom and I had gone to New York City on our honeymoon, and he'd surprised me with tickets to *Saturday Night Live*. The cards they used were just like these.

But I wasn't acting. I wasn't performing. The key here was to speak from my heart.

The red light on the camera glowed, and I smiled into the lens. "My name is Anita Brown. And I am a member of Joyful Justice. I'm a killer, and I'm a victim, and I am a woman...a daughter and a sister."

I took in a slow deep breath, a calm coming over me. "It wasn't that long ago that I fought for justice within the confines of society. I worked as an investigative reporter, and I exposed wrongdoers to the light. That's when I thought that light could solve everything. Shine light into darkness, and the truth is revealed."

I shook my head. "But the fact is that in that darkness lurks the power that controls this world. It's not the darkness of society but the darkness of our own minds. The cultures that we have formed as people. They're outdated; they're wrong."

"After I was attacked, while I was recovering, I asked myself if I was wrong to kill the man who had held me captive for days, raped me, burned me." I held out my arm, exposing the scars there. Goosebumps raised on my skin. To be revealing those scars was at once terrifying and liberating, like leaping from a plane knowing I had a parachute on my back.

Tom, and Dan, and the rest of the people in my life were that parachute. I could always pull the string, and they would help ease my fall.

I plummeted toward the ground, planning to land on my own two feet.

CHAPTER TWENTY-ONE
ENDINGS ARE OFTEN BEGINNINGS

Mulberry

The Florida sunlight poured in through the windows, caressing Sandy where she sat in a burgundy vinyl armchair, looking out at the view. We couldn't quite see the ocean but the glass towers of Miami were impressive in their own way.

"What do you think?" I asked.

She started and turned toward me, a smile chasing away the moment of fear. Her grin grew larger as she took me in. I was up on crutches, walking around—well, hobbling, but a hell of a lot better than I'd been.

"You look great," she said, crossing the room to me. The hospital was more like a hotel, everything arranged for by Lenox.

Nothing but the best for you, my friend, he'd assured me.

Sandy put her arms around my neck for a hug. I awkwardly placed a hand on her back, careful to keep my balance and the crutches in place. She pulled back, her face tilting up to me, her body still pressed to mine.

Our gazes met, and it was like no time had passed, as though the clock had stopped that morning before I left for work, before I was shot. She lifted onto her tiptoes, and I bent my head. Our lips met in a tentative kiss—both of us scared, if hopeful.

Her tongue caressed my lips, and I moaned, pulling her closer, one of my crutches tumbling to the ground with a clatter that pulled us apart.

She kept a steadying hand on me, her eyes down on the crutch.

My heart thudded in my chest. "I'm different," I said.

She smiled and didn't look up at me. "You don't even remember the past ten years. You could, at any moment, and who knows what you'll think then." Her eyes came up to mine—as bright and blue as the sky outside.

"Clearly I was a fool. I let you go back then. And now I've gotten my leg blown off." She gave me a small laugh. We could joke about my injury...we belonged together. "Be my family, again."

Sandy narrowed her eyes. "How about I be your girlfriend, first?"

"You mean it?" My voice sounded high. She nodded, her cheeks glowing pink. I pulled her close, covering her mouth with mine. She moaned, and I twisted to rest her back against the wall, using it to steady us both. Her hands explored my shoulders, ran up into my hair.

I felt a shiver on the back of my neck and broke the kiss, turning toward the door.

A window out into the hall was empty—no one was watching. But I could have sworn...

Sandy pulled me back to her, and I fell into the kiss, into her. Into my past and my future.

$$EK$$

April

Robin's-egg blue cloth draped the edge of the stage, and the choir wore matching robes—it all matched Nicholas's eyes. His suit shone under the bright lights as he paced behind the pulpit, bringing the crowd up to a frothy mix.

It was almost like watching water boil: those first few bubbles almost shyly rising to the surface, the early signs that a rolling boil would soon erupt. By the time he introduced me, the crowd was a sputtering, heated mass of excitement.

They were ready to hear the word. Ready to hear how I could take them to new heights. I stepped out onto the stage, and the lights hit me. I blinked against them, but did not look away.

This was so much bigger than the small churches and communities I'd been moving through. This was what I had been working for. As I stepped behind the pulpit, Nicholas put his arm around my waist and leaned over to kiss my cheek. He whispered into my ear. "They're all yours."

His hand dipped down from my waist and squeezed my ass. A little sound of surprise left me, and he winked before striding away. I turned to the crowd, the imprint of his hand burning on my butt.

"Good evening," I said. The crowd yelled back a greeting. I took a deep breath, clearing my mind. *Nothing could stop me now.*

"I'm here to tell you a story." The crowd began to settle. "A story you may have heard before. Perhaps you've seen some of my videos. Perhaps you've read about me online."

The audience murmured; they had heard of me. My message had already reached them. *This was just the live show.*

I released the microphone from its stand and stepped out from behind the pulpit, clearing my mind of everything but what needed to happen.

"We all decide our own value."

My voice rang out over the crowd, and another sound rang out behind it. A popping sound. I felt a sharp pain in my side.

I doubled over, suddenly looking at the wooden boards of the stage.

Another pop and I twisted, falling onto my back, finding it difficult to breathe.

Screaming erupted as more popping sounds echoed.

Gunshots.

I raised my head, looking down at myself, and saw blood. There was blood pumping out of a wound in my stomach and more streaming down my arm.

And then the pain came, washing over me, constricting my chest—I struggled to breathe through it. A rasping gurgle filled my head.

And then there were faces above me. People yelling. A medic—the red cross on his uniform brighter than the blood staining my dress.

My eyes slipped closed, and all I could hear was the rushing of blood in my ears, the loud thumping of my heart.

I was still alive.

"Move her, move her!" I heard yelling. My body was lifted, pain slicing through me. I heard myself groan, and my eyes opened at the impact of my body being put onto a stretcher.

They were wheeling me when Cynthia appeared by my side, her hand lacing into mine. Her face hovered over me, tears streaming down her cheeks.

My eyes began to close again. "Please, please!" Cynthia cried. "Don't go. Stay with me."

The devil whispered, and God sighed, and I recognized that my faith in Him, my faith in *Her*, my faith in Cynthia, all led to this. But I didn't know where this was leading.

EK

Robert

Sydney Rye stood on the deck of my home on an island in Miami's Biscayne Bay, her back to me, Blue and two of his puppies standing next to her as she stared out at the ocean. The sunset cast a pink glow over the whole world, making it look sweet and peaceful, a mirage that I wanted to make true for her.

The sound of waves lapping at the shore reached into my living room. Did the sound calm her, as it did me?

The door behind me opened, and I turned to see Merl entering the large space, his footfalls silent even on the marble steps. The man was a ninja, all wiry muscle and controlled strength coupled with remarkable skill. Merl's morals, his sense of justice, steered him as true and steady as a compass needle pulled north. This made him easy to predict. He posed no danger to me.

My gaze was pulled back to Sydney. The wind played with her hair, making it dance around her neckline.

Her heart was broken.

Peering through that window into Mulberry's room, we'd seen him kissing his ex-wife. And, wow, what a kiss.

"He doesn't remember you," Lenox told her. There was a beat of silence as she continued to stare, to spy on the intimate moment.

Then she'd turned away. "It's better if he never does." And she'd strode back down the hall, her back straight, her face a mask of indifference, but I knew that pain radiated through her.

Merl came to stand next to me now, his eyes on Sydney as well. "How is she today?" he asked. Merl had flown in the day before, here to help oversee Sydney's care.

Because I couldn't be trusted.

"Quiet," I answered. Merl nodded, but didn't speak. "She's been out there most of the day."

"And you've been here?" he asked. "Watching her?"

"Something like that," I admitted.

"The therapist came today?"

"Yes."

"Dan says he's the best."

Like I would ever work with anyone who wasn't. "Yes, I've known him for some time." *He owes me.*

Merl watched me, his eyes sharp. I turned to meet his gaze. "Something about you is different."

My brows rose. "Is it?"

His eyes narrowed, inspecting me. I let him look. "It's like...you want to take care of her, instead of control her."

Insightful little shit.

I forced a smile onto my face. "I don't know what you're talking about. I've always wanted to help."

Merl shook his head. "No, you're different." He grinned, exposing gapped front teeth. "You're—"

"Enough," I barked. "I'm not the one in therapy."

He laughed, and my hand clenched into a fist.

"No, but you're different anyway."

Merl's phone rang, and his face lit up when he looked at the screen. *Must be his girlfriend.* He stepped away to answer it. He spoke in Mandarin Chinese, a language I studied but wasn't fluent in yet.

My own phone rang, and I pulled it from my pocket. *One of my contacts at the police department.* "Yes."

"Mr. Maxim, I have some information for you."

"Go on."

"April Madden was shot at an evangelical revival."

"When and where?" I kept my voice steady even as my heart rate picked up.

"Just now, sir, about fifteen minutes ago. In Fort Lauderdale."

"Is she alive?"

"On last report. She's on her way to the hospital."

"Keep me updated."

"Yes, sir."

I slipped my phone back into my pocket and returned my attention to Sydney.

Merl came back, his long ponytail swinging with each stride. *He didn't know about April.* But he would soon. Dan would too. And he'd tell Sydney.

But for right now, in this moment, I'd keep Sydney safe. Keep her free of worry and pain. *She was finally under my care.*

EK

Sydney

Blue leaned against my side, releasing a low sigh. His puppies, whom I'd named Nila and Frank, slept on the wooden deck.

Nila, the word for 'dark blue' in Sanskrit, was the smallest of the litter, her eyes the same rich aqua as the bay before me. Frank, the only pup with his father's mismatched eyes, was also the biggest...and I was starting to think the dumbest. Named after my father, he ate like a beast and had only learned to sit, while Nila could heel, lie down, and stay. Hopefully he would learn in time.

Something to work for, something to live for.

Their soft snoring brought me comfort and purpose.

Robert Maxim's gaze on my back felt like a blanket around my shoulders, one both protective and stifling.

Mulberry kissing his wife, his hand at her waist, his face bent to hers, the way she molded to him like they belonged together, kept flashing through my mind—a knife stabbing into my chest. My heart ached for my own loss, but also celebrated for him. Everything we'd been through together, all the pain, the adventure, the disappointments...it was all wiped out for him. *He got a fresh start.*

Maybe I could have one, too.

Could I, perhaps, become someone else? Someone healthy, happy, and normal?

A laugh bubbled in my chest as I imagined myself rollerblading along the ocean path in Miami Beach, Blue and his puppies racing alongside me. *It didn't seem possible.*

But it wasn't so long ago that I wouldn't have conceived of killing, of fighting for justice. I just wanted my takeout and TV, to pay the rent and have fun with my friends...with my brother.

James's face floated through my mind, pushing aside the painful image of Mulberry. James's infectious laugh reverberated in my head. To think of him no longer hurt.

A revelation.

Time heals all.

Maybe even me.

Lightning cracked across my vision, and I gripped the railing of the deck as a harsh voice whispered into my mind. *You can run, but you will never escape me. I am you. I am* Her.

We are not done yet.

EK

Turn the page to read an excerpt from

Betray the Lie, Sydney Rye Mysteries Book 11, or purchase it now and continue reading Sydney's next adventure:
emilykimelman.com/BL

EK

Sign up for my newsletter and stay up to date on new releases, free books, and giveaways:
emilykimelman.com/News

Join my Facebook group, *Emily Kimelman's Insatiable Readers,* to stay up to date on sales and releases, have exclusive giveaways, and hang out with your fellow book addicts: emilykimelman.com/EKIR.

SNEAK PEEK
BETRAY THE LIE, SYDNEY RYE MYSTERIES
BOOK 11

Declan

Five years. I've been waiting five years for this moment. And now here I am. Standing behind my men, controlling them with the microphone at my mouth. Sydney Rye, aka Joy Humbolt, will not escape. I've got the warrant. I've got the man power. We are on US territory.

I will defeat her.

The pounding of Fermont's fist against the mansion's door echoes inside Robert Maxim's giant, modern Miami residence on Star Island. From the road, all you can see are white walls fronted with lush tropical gardens, but on the ocean side it's all glass.

The guy lives quite the life.

He offered me a job years ago—tried to lure me away from the New York police force right as I made Detective. I thought I'd go. Figured I'd make a killing.

But then...Joy Humbolt. She upended my life. Instead of being the easy, fast, fun fuck I wanted her to be, she turned out to be a goddamn assassin. She humiliated me....made me into a fool.

After murdering her brother's killer in New York, she went on the run; but her act of vengeance—those few bullets sunk into a man's chest

—spawned a movement. Joyful Justice, a vigilante network that started as an online forum, soon mutated into an international fighting force causing havoc around the world. *Taking justice into their own hands and making headlines doing it.*

Robert Maxim protected her all these years. *Fuck that.* I'm bringing them both down, then I'll destroy the rest of Joyful Justice one member at a time. But I need to stay calm now, in this moment of victory.

No one answers the door, so I call for the battering ram. The team moves in seamless formation. The ram appears, the men swing it back and smash into the mahogany doors. Once...twice...on the third time, the big frame lets go and the door swings in. My men pour forth: black, armored warriors here to save the day.

I follow in their wake, my weapon up, the weight of my equipment making me sweat in the warm night.

I doubt Robert will try to fight his way out of the house. He's too slick for that.

It took me five judges to find one who would write the warrant, but I found one. *I always win.*

EK

Sydney

The doors to the secret elevator, open and a voice behind us yells, "Freeze. Now!" Glancing back, I see three men in the living room, their weapons raised, the matte black of their helmets absorbing the last rays of the sun set.

With the elevator doors open, on the precipice of escape, Robert and I freeze, our bodies stilling. *The calm before the storm.*

Blue growls, and Frank gives off a deep bark of excitement. Nila presses against my leg, waiting for a command.

"Turn around slowly," the man orders.

Robert releases my hand, and we both turn to face the armed intruders, joined now by two more. Their radios crackle. Bodies hunched around their weapons, the heavy armor they wear under their uniforms making them sweat, they keep their rifles aimed at our chests.

A strong gust of wind puffs through the open glass doors, bringing the briny scent of the sea. I take a deep breath. *I love that smell.*

My hands are up, Robert's, too. But we are not surrendering. That's not what Robert and I do.

Declan Doyle pauses at the top of the four steps leading down into the living room. His brown eyes land on mine. A smile, predatory and satisfied, leaps into his gaze—the look of a wolf whose crept into the center of the sheep herd. Declan thinks he's about to feast.

Poor Declan Doyle, so wrong, so often.

A small hint of sympathy curls in my stomach considering what it must be like to pursue someone so desperately, to believe in one moment you've captured them, only to lose them again in the next.

Parting is such sweet sorrow...for one of us anyway.

"Sydney," Declan says.

I nod. "Declan, how are you?"

He starts down the steps. "Better than you."

"Perhaps, but I have been well recently. How has your recovery been?"

His face darkens, and his hand brushes against his side where I shot him. "I'm fine."

"Hello, Declan," Robert says. "Making more terrible career choices, I see."

Declan glances at Robert for only a moment before returning his attention to me. "I wouldn't take career advice from him," Declan says to me. "Could land you in jail." He grins. "Oh right, you're going there anyway."

Robert huffs a laugh but does not speak.

Declan frowns and then, looking down at Blue, a smile crosses his face. "It's a shame," he says. "If those dogs don't come easy. They will be put down."

"Declan," I say. "Do you really need to threaten my dogs? Aren't you bigger than that?"

. . .

"Besides," Robert says, shrugging. "I've never seen threatening Blue go well. For anyone. Ever."

Declan looks over at Robert. "Well, Robert Maxim, things are changing."

Robert smiles, slow and scary, like he knows so much more than anyone else in the room...hell, anyone else in the world. "The more things change the more they stay the same," Robert says it quietly, almost humbly...if it wasn't for the glee in his gaze.

"Not this time, Robert," Declan says, his own smug smile pulling at his lips.

A sigh escapes me as the two men's egos clash. *The ego is to be transcended, not bargained with or defeated.*

Declan turns on his heel. "Cuff and ready them for transport," he says to one of his men as he heads back out to the hall.

Sympathy wells in me for one more moment as I watch his broad back leave the room. *He won't even be here to witness his defeat.*

$$EK$$

Continue reading *Betray the Lie*: emilykimelman.com/BL

$$EK$$

Sign up for my newsletter and stay up to date on new releases, free books, and giveaways:
emilykimelman.com/News

Join my Facebook group, *Emily Kimelman's Insatiable Readers,* **to stay up to date on sales and releases, have exclusive giveaways, and hang out with your fellow book addicts:** emilykimelman.com/EKIR.

AUTHOR'S NOTE

Thank you for reading *Flock of Wolves*. I'm excited that you made it to my note. I'm guessing that means that you enjoyed my story. If so, would you please write a review for *Flock of Wolves*? You have no idea how much it warms my heart to get a new review. And this isn't just for me, mind you. Think of all the people out there who need reviews to make decisions. The children who need to be told this book is not for them. And the people about to go away on vacation who could have so much fun reading this on the plane. Consider it an act of kindness to me, to the children, to humanity.

Let people know what you thought about *Flock of Wolves* on your favorite ebook retailer.

Thank you,

Emily

ABOUT THE AUTHOR

I write because I love to read...but I have specific tastes. I love to spend time in fictional worlds where justice is exacted with a vengeance. Give me raw stories with a protagonist who feels like a friend, heroic pets, plots that come together with a BANG, and long series so the adventure can continue. If you got this far in my book then I'm assuming you feel the same...

Sign up for my newsletter and
never miss a new release or sale:
emilykimelman.com/News

Join my Facebook group, *Emily Kimelman's Insatiable Readers,* to stay up to date on sales and releases, have exclusive giveaways, and hang out with your fellow book addicts: emilykimelman.com/EKIR.

If you've read my work and want to get in touch please do! I loves hearing from readers.
www.emilykimelman.com
emily@emilykimelman.com

facebook.com/EmilyKimelman
instagram.com/emilykimelman

EMILY'S BOOKSHELF

Visit www.emilykimelman.com to purchase your next adventure.

EMILY KIMELMAN

MYSTERIES & THRILLERS

Sydney Rye Mysteries

Unleashed

Death in the Dark

Insatiable

Strings of Glass

Devil's Breath

Inviting Fire

Shadow Harvest

Girl with the Gun

In Sheep's Clothing

Flock of Wolves

Betray the Lie

Savage Grace

Blind Vigilance

Fatal Breach

Undefeated

Relentless

Brutal Mercy

Starstruck Thrillers

A Spy Is Born

EMILY REED

URBAN FANTASY

Kiss Chronicles

Lost Secret

Dark Secret

Stolen Secret

Buried Secret

Date TBA

Lost Wolf Legends

Butterfly Bones

Date TBA

Made in the USA
Middletown, DE
20 May 2024

54598140R10137